IN THE DARK

A hand shot out of the dark and wrapped around Kaylee's face, groping for her mouth before she could make a sound. Another strong arm grabbed her around her middle, yanking her backwards.

"It's me," she heard a familiar voice whisper in her ear. "Don't say any—*oof!*" Kaylee's self-defense training took over. Her brain recognized Ramon's voice immediately, but her elbow had already begun swinging back and up into her attacker's ribcage. Her father would have been glad to know the move worked; Ramon staggered back, gagging, until Kaylee heard him thump against the stairwell.

She whirled around and fumbled in space until she found him crouched in a fetal position. "*Dio!*" he wheezed, his voice barely a whisper.

PRAISE FOR NAOMI NASH!

BEANER O'BRIAN'S ABSOLUTELY GINORMOUS GUIDEBOOK TO GUYS

"This book is side-splitting funny! The story is attention-grabbing, and the book is sure to be a happy addition to your bookshelf. *Guidebook to Guys* is yet another out-of-the-park score for Naomi Nash."
—*Romance Reviews Today*

"A fun story."
—*RT BOOKclub*

"Naomi Nash has introduced us to many wonderful characters, but none have been as engaging and enjoyable to read about as Beaner O'Brian."
—Erika Sorocco, Teen Correspondent

"A great read."
—*The Best Reviews*

CHLOE, QUEEN OF DENIAL

"Smooch is setting the mark in quality young adult fiction, with this being no exception."
—*Huntress Reviews*

"Beautifully written, life-like, and features characters that really pull you into the story."
—*Romance Reviews Today*

YOU ARE SO CURSED!

"This book perfectly describes an alienated teenager in the hostile environment of high school. This tale is perfect for library shelves."
—*KLIATT*

"How can you go wrong with a book about a faux witch, a hot guy, a poop-crazy goat and those girls you just love to hate? ...This book finds a hilarious medium. Definitely recommended for the confused person in all of us."
—*RT BOOKclub*

SENSES WORKING OVERTIME

NAOMI NASH

SMOOCH NEW YORK CITY

SMOOCH ®

July 2005

Published by

Dorchester Publishing Co., Inc.
200 Madison Avenue
New York, NY 10016

ISBN 0-8439-5404-3

Printed in the United States of America.

Visit us on the web at www.smoochya.com.

ACKNOWLEDGMENTS

When I first learned to drive, I would jerk the steering wheel back and forth as I fretted about every potential hazard in my immediate path. Finally, probably tired of the herky-jerky experience, the wise man coaching me said, "Steer toward the horizon, and let the obstacles take care of themselves." It was such good advice that I've used it as my personal motto ever since. For the advice, I thank that wise driving instructor—my father, Alan.

SENSES WORKING OVERTIME

11:47 A.M.

"So, are you one?" Like a knife through silk, the unfamiliar boy's voice sliced through the silence.

People weren't supposed to talk in elevators, thought Kaylee. Certain things about the world never changed. The sun rose in the east and set in the west. The squared length of a right triangle's hypotenuse always equaled the squared length of both its other sides. None of her favorite bands ever made the Top Forty. Life always handed Kaylee Glass the short end of the stick.

And in crowded elevators, people faced the front, held their hands at their sides, kept their eyes glued to the flickering display of floor numbers, and never, ever spoke aloud. Yet something about the boy's voice intrigued her. When Kaylee turned to look, Carl squeezed her shoulder with a scarlet-tinged grip, reminding her to keep still. More than anything in the world she wanted to wrench away, but she couldn't. She would escape—and soon. But not yet.

If Carl hadn't been so much on her mind, she might

have turned her entire head to check out the boy. He was trouble. Kaylee could tell that much merely from the corners of her eyes. He sprawled against the side handrail, legs spread wide so he occupied the space of three people. He seemed handsome, yes. The way his sleeveless red t-shirt showed off the dark skin of his considerable biceps and shoulders made him almost kind of . . . well, hot. You might even call the boy interesting, but from the way he was disregarding the Rules of the Elevator, she would bet any amount of money he was nothing but trouble.

"Hey." The boy poked at the back of her knee with one of his feet. Kaylee's eyes immediately snapped down from the safe zone above the bald man's head in front of her. Through a hole in the boy's red Converse high-tops, she could see most of his big toe. "So, *are* you one?"

He'd been talking to her? Kaylee flushed. She was used to no one ever paying her any attention. Though the grip on her shoulder intensified, she spoke boldly anyway. She wasn't Carl's to control. "Am I one what?" Including Carl and herself, there must have been ten people packed into those four walls of smooth steel paneling. In such close quarters, her voice sounded unnaturally loud. Could everyone hear how strained she seemed?

The bell chimed softly; a digital display showed the number 42. The metal doors slid open with a soft rush of sound. "Excuse me." A middle-aged woman pushed her way past, her voice annoyed and tired.

"Going down?" asked a short man immediately outside. Once the grumpy woman had vanished, he stepped in. First he adjusted his cuff links and smoothed down his suit in a fussy manner. Then, as the doors closed, he attended to his tie and checked his collar.

The kid needed a haircut badly. Heck, his dark, thick hair had needed shearing three months ago. He nodded in Kaylee's direction, eyes squarely on her breasts. "You know."

What a pig! What kind of a perv stared in public at a girl's . . . oh. His eyes had been scanning the T-shirt her dad had given her as a sixteenth birthday present four months before. Glitter letters across its khaki green front spelled two words: *ARMY PRINCESS*.

Without meeting the boy's gaze, Kaylee tugged at the shirt's hem. Even though the most that showed was her navel, his interest made her feel almost naked. "Oh, am I an army princess? Nope." Princesses were perfect; princesses did as they pleased. A princess wouldn't have ended up trapped in downtown Manhattan on the hottest day of the year, looking for a way to escape from the slimiest boy she'd ever known. Not when she was supposed to be cooling her heels in air-conditioned summer school classrooms so she could rejoin the junior class come autumn. "I mean, my mom and dad are in the military, but . . . "

"Hey." Carl had been squeezing her shoulder the entire time she'd talked, but now he gave her a vicious pinch—dark purple, the color of a bruise—that cut short her words. Carl put his arm completely around her shoulders, clutching Kaylee closer. "I said, hey! Mexican kid!" he barked. "Why don't you try shuttin' up?" The adults around them shifted uneasily, as if worried some kind of fight might break out.

Carl was a bully. He and his girlfriend, Annabelle, both. He'd called the shots from the moment he'd surprised her upstairs in his father's empty office, when he'd pinned her against the wall and revealed exactly how thoroughly he and Annabelle had tricked her. Kaylee hated bullies. For a minute, the unknown boy had made her lose focus, but she needed to concentrate on her escape. She was smart. She could do it. If Carl had two brain cells to rub together, he could have written his own term papers and the whole mess that had ended with Kaylee being expelled from Westchester Country Day could have been avoided. Changing the past was impossible, but she could keep history from repeating itself. So she'd keep her mouth shut and act as if they were going to get money from her dad's account, just as she'd pretended to promise.

When they reached the lobby, she'd make a break for it. She'd run fast and hope she could outrace or outwit him. And this time, Kaylee swore by everything that meant anything, she'd never look back. She'd known Carl was bad news, but now that she knew the truth about Annabelle as well, she'd make sure they stayed out of her life for good. Only a few more minutes and Kaylee could go hurry home across the River and pretend she'd never taken today's detour, she reassured herself. Only a while more, and her dad would never know she'd nearly been hoodwinked into extracting money from his bank account. She patted the stolen ATM card in her pocket to make sure it was still there.

"No harm, no foul, man." The boy had raised his hands at Carl's rebuke. "Mexican, Cuban . . . either way, I still wasn't tryin' to chat up your girlfriend or nothin'."

Forget following the Rules of the Elevator. Kaylee had to protest that assumption. "He's *not* . . . "

"Listen, you little punk." Mr. Fussy Suit flinched at Carl's voice, his already bulging eyes swelling out farther. Though hard to tell when the boy was slumped down with his legs sprawled, Carl was easily the taller of the two, even towering over the adults in the elevator. He was all bulk, while the other boy was lean muscle. "Just shut the f—"

Kaylee smelled sour danger milliseconds before the elevator lights flickered. The electrical sound preceding their wild blinking left a vinegary taste on the back of her tongue and prickled her spine. The elevator stuttered up and down, then jerked to a stop beneath her feet, causing everyone around her to steady themselves with outspread arms. Even Carl let go of her shoulder to grab at the rail. Before Kaylee could consider how to react, the ceiling lights guttered out.

The elevator car plunged into darkness.

No one in the car made a peep in the seconds that followed. To Kaylee, it sounded as if the immense building was a motor slowly powering down. Over the thudding of her heart, she could barely make out its last dying whine. They were trapped somewhere in the skyscraper's bowels, encased in a metal box suspended hundreds and hundreds of feet above the ground, confined in a space that seemed darker than night. Wasn't there supposed to be an emergency bulb? She wanted to scream, yell, stamp her feet—anything to drive away the awful blackness. Why did disaster always have to happen to her? Why hadn't she ignored the telephone that morning on her way out the door?

As suddenly as the lights had disappeared, they flickered back on, almost painfully bright. Kaylee discovered she had turned sideways in her panic; to her relief, another woman had stepped backward between herself and Carl. Kaylee saw him whip his head around, but he couldn't grab her without pushing the businesswoman out of the way. Kaylee wasn't free, but every inch separating her from Carl would give her that much more of a head start when the moment came to run. The thought gave her hope.

She wasn't the only one in the elevator who'd moved. Half the men and women had lost their bearings during the seconds-long blackout and now faced in all directions but the front. The boy stared directly at her, his expression startled and frozen. Then his muscles relaxed. His tense lips spread into a slow, lazy grin, as if he and Kaylee shared some private joke. The elevator moved once more, continuing downward in a smooth path to the ground floor. "Close one, huh?" he said. Yeah, she realized. He really was good-looking. In a music video, he'd be cast as the bad boy out to have a good time, the guy almost too delicious to resist. But no—she couldn't afford to lose focus. She already had one bad boy muscling her down to the lobby. The kid spoke. "I don't know about you, but I'm gettin' off at the next floor."

"Why?" Although the little businessman had adjusted his collar moments before, he now crooked his index finger and ran it around the inside to give his neck some breathing space as he talked. "What do you know? What are you saying?" The man's bulging eyes darted around wildly, from the numbers above to the panel's lit-up buttons to the boy's face and then to the other passengers. Kaylee had once had a pet hamster that became frantic in the tight quarters of its hamster ball. The only difference between the twitching businessman and Sasquatch Jr. were whiskers and a pile of wood shavings. "I'm sure everything's okay now, right? Right?"

The boy curled his lip. "Bro, you can volunteer to stay in a hot metal box after the lights go out, but I'm not gonna take the chance."

"It was just a momentary blip." The man in the suit squeezed his eyes tightly shut, then blinked them open. Maybe his contact lenses were dry? "We'll be okay." His wedding band nervously rapped against the handrail.

The boy's shoulders rose and fell in a shrug. "If you say so, man." Kaylee hadn't been convinced by the adult's bluster either. The electricity's flickering had left the back of her mouth tasting both salty and sour—if she hadn't been surrounded by people, she would have gagged on her own saliva.

Once again the bell chimed, barely audible over the hollow *tap-tap-tap-tap-tap* of the businessman's ring finger. The woman separating Kaylee from Carl sighed at the noise and cast an irritated glance in the short man's direction. The doors slid open on the thirty-fifth floor, revealing a receptionist's desk and a swooping logo for the Versatekk Corporation. A tall woman in a tailored suit stepped quickly from the elevator, leather briefcase swinging. The brown-haired receptionist smiled with recognition as the woman slid smoothly by.

Right as the doors started to close, the boy followed, swaying from side to side as if he had all the time in the world. In his T-shirt with the arms cut off, high-top sneakers, and light brown shorts that hid half his calves, he looked woefully out of place against Versatekk's streamlined office furniture. The doors jerked again with a mechanical complaint, wanting to shut, but the boy held them apart so he could address Kaylee. "You coming?" he asked, his deep brown eyes staring right into her own.

For the first time since she'd entered the building, Kaylee felt a jolt of hope. Was this the opportunity she'd been looking for? She despised feeling jailed and confined—she hated it from her parents but disliked it even more from Carl, the guy who'd already landed her in a mess of trouble. Was this her chance at escape? Or would she be leaping from the frying pan into the fire? She couldn't see herself taking chances with a street thug.

Yet his two words—*you coming?*—had smelled almost sweet. Not overpowering, like strong cologne. Gentle and oddly familiar, like a flower she'd once known. In her head, she could picture the blossoms, small and delicate, more white than yellow. . . .

"Kaylee's not going anywhere with you." Carl's finger shot out and jabbed at a button. Once more the inner workings of the door started to glide shut, and once more the boy's quick hand reversed them.

"Are you comin'?" repeated the boy. His head inclined toward Kaylee. She had to make a decision.

Tap-tap-tap-tap-tap. Before she could shake her head, the nervous little man bolted out. "If she's not, I will," he said, barreling forward. Again he attempted to loosen the neck of his crisp white shirt. "This is a freakin' nightmare," he murmured.

The elevator's remaining occupants all seemed relieved that the man had left, taking his nervous tapping with him. "Your choice," said the boy. His eyes never left hers. His brown fingers skimmed down the metal, finally releasing the doors.

"About time, jerkwad!" Carl snapped, his words red and angry against the back of Kaylee's neck. The doors started to glide together.

Honeysuckle. That had been the flower—honeysuckle. Its yellow-white blooms had overgrown the chain-link fence of their home in Quantico, five years ago. At the time it had been one of her most favorite smells in the world. All of Kaylee's unusual senses seemed to urge her to take the chance. For once, she listened to them. "Wait!"

The elevator doors had half shut by the time she moved forward. Would she make it through? An arm reached out and pulled her out—the boy's hand tightly held her own and yanked her from the elevator into the air-conditioned cool of the thirty-fifth floor. She barely had time to whirl around and see Carl's face, scarlet and furious, as once more he dove for the button panel.

The doors closed. Kaylee held her breath. Would they open again? No, she prayed. Please, no.

The seam remained shut. The moment she was separated from Carl by a door of solid metal that even his bad temper couldn't penetrate, her doubt blossomed into relief. She'd done it. She'd ditched him! Kaylee wasn't foolish enough to think that she was safe yet, at least not until she was on her way back to Brooklyn. Yet she'd taken the leap. Her ordeal was almost over, and all because of words that had smelled of summer flowers.

"Man, that boyfriend of yours is the jerkwad." Was she still holding the stranger's hand? She reclaimed her fingers and shook them. "What're you doin' with a sleazeball boyfriend like him, huh?" he asked.

Kaylee opened her mouth in angry protest. "He's *not* my boyfriend!" Once more her mouth filled with that sour metallic taste. Above them, the lights flickered, the fluorescent bulbs snapping and crackling as they flashed out an urgent distress signal.

"Aw, crap, not again!" moaned the little businessman, his bug eyes turning upward.

Then the lights went out for good.

11:51 A.M.

"The building . . . encing a power outage. Please pro-cee . . . exit. The building . . . " Over and over, a tinny recorded voice hissed from loudspeakers somewhere in the ceiling, barely audible over a sea of static.

"Oh, this so isn't happening." The man in the business suit paced back and forth, each step of his shiny leather shoes clicking against the marble tiles where they stood. "This can't be—crap! Not now. Not to me!"

"Try to chillax a little, bro. You'll live longer."

The boy sounded irritated, but Kaylee was squarely on the man's side. She would have said so if the snap and crackle of the lights hadn't left her mouth flooded with sour saliva. This mess couldn't be happening to her. Not today. Once again, Carl and her former friend Annabelle had left her the victim of what her dad would have called a pretty sticky situation. That had been the phrase he'd used in the principal's office last May, when she'd been expelled. *This is a pret-ty sticky*

11

situation, sweetpea, he'd said, disappointment plain in his eyes. *Pret-ty sticky.*

Sticky. Some understatement! She'd been totally grounded for the entire summer, confined to school and her bedroom. And here Kaylee stood, stranded in a city she didn't know, high in a building with the lights out, miles from home and from the class where she was supposed to be reviewing sine and cosine rules. Sticky didn't begin to describe it—she'd been dumped into a pit with syrup-smeared walls and a floor spread with Krazy Glue. Her mom was out of town today, thank God, but after all the promises she'd made to keep out of trouble, how could she face her dad again? She had to get home before he did.

The boy's voice interrupted her thoughts. "Hey, you okay?" Kaylee opened her eyes. How long had she been sitting on her knees? "You havin' some kind of panic attack or something? What's up? Hey . . . "

Again, his words smelled of honeysuckle. Gagging from the spit in her mouth, she held up a finger. "Sh-sh-shneesha," she tried. It took all her energy to make one enormous gulp and choke down the excess dribble. "Synesthesia," she said more clearly. She hadn't expected him to recognize the word; no one did. Even her parents and friends barely believed in the strange ways she sometimes experienced the world.

The boy made an expression of aversion. "Is that like, contagious or something? 'Cause I ain't lookin' to visit no doctor. I was just tryin' to help." He knelt down beside her and repeated his original question. "You okay?"

Kaylee didn't care when people flinched away from

the long Latin word. She'd been used to that for years, ever since the first army neurologist had told her parents why certain sounds made her think she smelled scents no one else smelled, or why textures and sensations against her skin seemed to suggest certain colors. When she tried to regain her feet, he offered her an arm. She ignored it.

"It's a harmless condition," she told the boy, taking a moment to regain her balance. A curse, more like. Not for the first time, Kaylee wished she could live a normal life like every other girl she knew. "My brain links senses together weirdly, that's all. Like, sometimes when I hear a noise, my brain sends extra signals to my tongue. So when the lights went out, I got this bad taste in my mouth. That's all." Probably best not to mention the smell that had convinced her to exit the elevator moments before.

She still was grateful for that phantom scent. If she'd stayed by Carl's side, she'd at this moment be in that airless metal box, suspended hundreds of feet over nothing. Part of her smirked at the thought of Carl trapped and caged somewhere around the thirty-first floor. Served him right! Most of her shuddered, though. The few seconds she had spent confined in that absolute blackness had been among the very worst of her life.

"The building . . . encing a power outage. Please procee . . . "

At least this floor wasn't completely dark. Although the wall behind the receptionist was solid, the glass and Lucite partitions beyond let in light from outside windows. The emergency exit lights had tripped while her eyes had been closed; it really wasn't that much darker than her own room at dusk, or during a particularly cloudy thunderstorm. "So you're okay?"

She should have known better than to open her mouth. "I told you the first time. Yes." Why did the boy keep looking at her? "I'm fine. Stop staring at me like I'm some kind of freak." Kaylee's condition wasn't life-threatening or dangerous. In fact, people with synesthesia often were highly intelligent and creative. It was just a part of her, like her red-brown hair or green eyes.

Yeah, he'd helped her make up her mind to get off the elevator. Considering where it was now, she was grateful. What did he want, though, a freaking medal? Forget it. She didn't have the time. If she started now, she could easily get back home before her dad's shift ended. All that stood between her and safety was a single subway train back to Brooklyn. She was about to wish the kid a nice life when he spoke again. "Ramon," he said. "That's my name." Once again his arm extended, offering help up.

He was persistent. She had to give him that. Grabbing onto his hand, she finally struggled up to her feet. "I'm . . . "

"Kaylee," he announced. Her obvious surprise made him laugh. "That big-headed friend of yours said it, remember? What'd you think I was, some kind of stalker? I'm a nice guy."

She couldn't help but let out a short laugh. "Carl does have a big head." And a big mouth to match. She wondered how he was coping. To escape him, all she had to do now was find a way out of the building before the lights came back on. Wouldn't that be the best justice of all, after all the trouble he'd caused? To vanish before he got the cash he and Annabelle had tried to squeeze from her? Well, maybe the best justice would involve the police, a runaway wild tiger, and a vat of boiling acid, but she'd settle for what she could get.

"The building . . . encing a power outage." If only they'd shut off the speakers! The static was driving Kaylee crazy.

Over by the receptionist's desk, the little man in the suit was making a scene. "You must have heard of Melano and Fruschette. Forty-second floor?" Despite the gloom, Kaylee could tell that the receptionist looked up at him with big, bored eyes. One of her fingers touched where a headset rested, as if she were on a call. The other hand sheltered her free ear from the static and chatter. "I'm Mr. Cloutier. Brody Cloutier? Of Acquisitions? I'm very well-known. Listen up: Call the building engineer right now and—"

"Yes, I'm still here," said the receptionist, suddenly. She must have been on hold. Kaylee wished she had a quarter of the woman's elegance. From her mouth, the most mundane words sounded sophisticated. "It certainly seems to be going around. They're out here, too."

"My wife—" Mr. Cloutier practically leaned over the desk to attract the receptionist's attention. She held up a single finger to arrest him in mid-speech.

"Really?" said the receptionist, shaking her head so that her hoop earrings glinted in the light of the emergency exits. "That *is* a weird coincidence. Yes, I can hold."

Ramon had wandered over to the desk a moment before. Some purple compulsion roused by the receptionist's reaction made Kaylee follow—apprehension? Fear? Ramon, though, didn't seem to share any of the sensations tickling at her insides. He leaned his dark-skinned arms over the counter, his body curling sleekly like a tiger's, and gave the receptionist a smile that seemed to expose nearly all his teeth. "Hey," he purred. "What's goin' on?"

"My wife—" Mr. Cloutier tried again.

"Nice guy, huh?" Kaylee said, shocked but not at all surprised. Ramon was trying to pick up a woman! She had to be at least twenty-seven! He probably *had* been staring at Kaylee's breasts, earlier. Weren't there any boys who had an off switch on their hormones? "You're a big player!" Then again, what more could she expect from a street thug?

The boy shot her a quelling look, but it didn't matter. The receptionist had already responded to the smile like a kitten to catnip. "One of our branches in Cleveland," she explained, pointing to the headset.

The receptionist grew chilly when Mr. Cloutier interrupted. "Listen, miss, I've got to get out of here. Don't you understand?" The little businessman's patience seemed to have evaporated. He leaned over the counter and grabbed for the phone, but the receptionist eased it out of reach. Kaylee noticed her expression didn't even change. "Call the building engineers, so they can get the power back on. . . . "

"Don't be actin' all crazy on the lady," said Ramon, plainly annoyed. "She's just doin' her job."

"And I'm try*ing* to get to my wife." Mr. Cloutier's

voice grew louder. Kaylee felt her hackles rise at the way he over-enunciated his *-ing*. Impatience was one thing—rudeness another. "My new wife. She's hav-*ing* a baby."

"Yours?" Kaylee blurted. The second the word left her lips she realized how terrible it must have sounded. Ramon laughed, then quickly shut his mouth and winked at her. Sorry, Charlie, Kaylee thought. Out of gratitude she might have risen to his defense for a minute, but she wasn't interested in players.

The little man's face turned red. "Of course it's mine! What's that supposed to mean? The point is—"

"The stairs are that way, sir." The receptionist pointed a long, painted nail in the direction of the elevator hallway, then used it again to press her headset against her ear. "Yes, I'm still here. And you're without power, too? How in the world did that happen?"

"Your buds in Cleveland don't have lights either?" Ramon asked, his eyebrows raised. The receptionist, still murmuring into the microphone that jutted toward her mouth, shrugged. With an incline of his shaggy head, Ramon looked in Kaylee's direction, as if trying to tell her something. "Wow. Whatta coincidence."

"That's not a coincidence." For the first time in five minutes, Mr. Cloutier stood still without twitching. "That's terrorism."

That particular word always sent black shivers up Kaylee's spine—the deep, hollow black of nightmares and disease. Her head turned, looking for a window. What if something horrible was happening outside? "Come on," Ramon said. "No way."

"With the electricity out from here to Cleveland?"

With every syllable, the man's voice grew more shrill. "They've hacked into the power plants. The electricity could be out all over the country for all we know. My wife!" For a quick second, Mr. Cloutier's frightening explanation alarmed her. Kaylee could have missed six years of school and she still would have known there were a lot of miles between Manhattan and Ohio. How could so many people all have lost power at the same time? Mr. Cloutier began to swear to himself.

"That's stupid, man," said Ramon. Why was he so casual about all this? How could she have been fooled by that false scent of honeysuckle? Her father would have disliked Ramon, with his sloppy clothes and attitude. "For one thing, no one said anything about power bein' out everywhere between here and there. Coincidence? Sure. It's a hot day. Terrorists? Nah."

He had a point. It could be a coincidence. Both cities could be experiencing their own smaller blackouts. What if they weren't localized, though? As panic started to claw its way from her stomach to her gullet, Ramon turned so that his mouth was positioned near her ear. Over the noise of the loudspeakers' crackling recorded announcement, he murmured, "Do you really want him to start a panic up here? Keep everybody happy, army princess."

Kaylee looked at Ramon with surprise. He was totally right. A panic would be disastrous. What if hundreds of terrified people clogged the stairwells and kept her from leaving the building? Okay, that thought was totally selfish, but nonetheless true. She had to help calm this guy down before he blew a gasket. "It can't be terrorists," she announced. Even the receptionist stopped talking to listen. "The power grid has too many fail-safes to be hacked into. The hacker thing only happens in movies."

"Yeah, that's what I said," Ramon agreed.

Mr. Cloutier looked astonished that she'd spoken at all. "How do you know?"

"Her dad's in the army," said Ramon, nodding at her with approval. "They know all about terrorists."

If it had been possible to ignore Ramon completely, she would have. But it was a good lead. "My mom is an electrical engineer," she admitted, then added a lie. "She's probably working on this right now." It was a good thing her mother was in South Carolina on a special assignment; otherwise she'd be totally freaking out in another hour and a half when Kaylee didn't arrive home. The absolute earliest her dad could be home would be seven—army air fields didn't close even during blizzards or nuclear explosions. A blackout would be nothing to them. She'd be home in plenty of time before then, though. "Listen, it's probably just a heatwave thing. It's pretty hot outside."

"But my wife's having a baby!"

"My man, listen up," said Ramon, abandoning the counter and sauntering over. "My mom, you know? She had my little sister in the middle of the living room floor when she couldn't get to the hospital in time. Right there on the *rug*. The mailman was stoppin' by and he was all like, 'Holy crap! What're you doin', lady?' and she was all like, 'Help me!' and stuff, so he got down and she yelled and pushed and then she had my little sister in like, his mailbag. It's okay, he emptied all the letters out first," he assured Kaylee.

"I'm glad," she said, because he seemed to want some kind of answer. She didn't want to prolong this conversation or anything.

"Yeah, there was like, blood all *over* the damn place and the mailman, he was close to faintin' because it was like, all smelly—"

Mr. Cloutier was looking decidedly queasy; his jaw hung slack. "Yeah, thanks," Kaylee snapped at Ramon. "Very helpful in the *keeping people happy department.*"

Ramon finished his story softly. "But the thing is, my sister turned out okay, even bein' born in the bag. Real okay."

"I'm sure she's okay," she added to Mr. Cloutier. "Your wife, I mean. Not his . . . anyway. Hospitals have those, you know. Backup generators." He nodded faintly, seeming calmer. Or maybe he was just stunned and picturing his baby looking up at him from a U.S. Postal Service bag. Either way, it was an ideal moment to make her exit and escape for good from this hellhole. "I bet she's fine." In his own twisted way, Ramon had been trying to reassure the man as well, of course. She'd been ruder than she should have been.

Oh, did it matter? It was time to go. She wouldn't see Ramon again. He could soothe any hurt feelings by flirting with all the ladies of Versatekk. "Later," she told him. As the maddening recording started up again, she wheeled around in the direction of the plastic sign displaying a stick figure walking on stairs.

She'd scurried down to the thirty-fourth floor by the time the boy caught up with her. The stairwell— broad, concrete, and oddly empty—echoed with the sound of their shoes slapping against the metal-edged steps. "Wait up," Ramon called out in words of sheer vanilla. Of all the people in the world, why did Kaylee's maladjusted brain associate sweet smells with someone she was already sick of? When she looked over her shoulder, not only was Ramon bounding down after her two stairs at a time, but Mr. Cloutier was trotting behind, determined not to be abandoned. "I said, wait up!"

Thirty-three. "What for?" If only there was some way to lose herself in the shadows! She was too easy to follow in the emergency floodlights.

"I got questions for you!"

Thirty-two. Six turns around the painted metal banister and already she was feeling a little dizzy. Her head throbbed from the polka dot sounds of echoing footsteps and the inescapable, scratchy recording. "What kind?"

"Just like, questions. Like, if that meathead isn't your boyfriend, do you got one?" Oh. That *so* figured. She kept skipping down the steps and let the back of her head do the talking. "Okay, okay, for serious this time. This thing you got. Sympa . . . "

"Synesthesia. And it's not a disease."

"I didn't say disease, all right? Did I? Nope. I said *thing.*" Ramon was obviously one of those guys who enjoyed scoring points. "So what's it like? Is it like ESPN?"

What the—? "The sports channel?" Thirty. Twenty-nine long flights to go.

"Nah, nah, you know, like readin' minds and all that. Extra . . . "

Oh. She would have laughed, but it felt a little cruel. Ramon was as distant from the kids of Westchester Country Day School as they came. "ESP. No. It's not like that at all. It's—well, you know how when you get Chinese food, you can order it mild or spicy? Most people get mild, right? Everything I taste, see, smell— it's all extra spicy, all the time, no matter what."

"I don't get into Chinese," he said. The fact that he missed her point altogether cemented Kaylee's opinion of him. A stupid thug, through and through.

The entry to the twenty-ninth floor stood wide open; a college-aged boy with his shirtsleeves rolled up leaned against the door to keep it open. Beyond, in a lobby, a number of businessmen and women milled about. "You going down to floor one?" he asked when Kaylee and her miniature entourage passed. "If you pass the elevator guys, would you tell them to hurry up?"

That stopped Kaylee cold. Ramon's elbows collided with her shoulder blades; Mr. Cloutier had to grab hold of the railing to prevent himself from slamming into them both. "You've got a stuck elevator on this floor?"

"Yeah. The folks inside are screaming and cussing like crazy," said the boy. "We heard there's another one trapped on twenty-four, but it only has a couple of people."

"Anyone actually hurt?" Kaylee asked.

The boy shrugged. "Nah. Just loud. I'd be loud, too, caught on one of those things."

Was it evil to hope she didn't see the elevator men on their way? All Kaylee wanted was a good head start home. She'd be safe once her own door was shut behind her. Carl wouldn't venture out to Brooklyn to find her—not with a dad at home who'd kick his butt if he dared show his face. Once more she began the dizzying spiral down. Barely had they rounded the next turn when Ramon's questions started again. "So you can't read minds, huh? What cool stuff can you do?"

"Why do you keep thinking it's cool?" Twenty-eight. "It's not cool at all."

"But you said it was like an extra sense. You already got five. That makes it your sixth sense, right? That's got to be something!"

Twenty-seven. Why did his words almost seem logical? "It's not *that* kind of sixth sense."

"But it's special, right? It sets you apart?"

For an entire lifetime, it had. "More than you know," she growled.

"So that's cool!" he said. When she glanced over her shoulder, his dark eyebrows had drawn up in a delighted arch. Kaylee believed he was sincere. She only wished she could share his enthusiasm. It would be nice if one person thought she was special, and not freakish. "No, seriously," he added. "I like special people. My sister's special."

Twenty-five. Her legs were tiring and so many changes of direction were making her head spin. "Because she was born in a mailbag?" Kaylee blurted out before she could stop herself. Why did she *say* things like that?

For a moment she heard nothing behind her, save Mr. Cloutier's nervous muttering. There were others ahead of them on their flight down now. A few of the people making their exodus from the building stepped quickly, bags slung over their shoulders, casting nervous glances upward as they descended. Others walked in slow pairs, talking to each other as if they had all the time in the world. Over the increased volume, it might have been difficult to hear Ramon if he'd answered. When Kaylee looked back, however, all she saw was the disappointed pout of his lips, and the downward arc of the scruffy hair on the top of his lip. "That was cold," he said, shaking his head. "You *know* it was cold, too."

"I didn't mean it that way." Twenty-two. So many flights to go, and already it felt as if she'd been on some crazy merry-go-round for longer than she could stand. "Look, could we just get out of here?"

"I'm not sayin' a thing more." Ramon's tone was hurt.

"Promise?"

"Fine. That's the last you'll hear from me," he said, contradicting himself mere seconds later with a mutter. "Wait 'til you need me for something, then we'll see how you like it when I'm cold right to *your* face. I'm gonna be an *iceberg.* And the look on your face when it happens? It's gonna be *money.*"

The mutters continued, not dying until they reached the eighteenth floor. By the time they were a dozen stories from the ground, the stairs were nearly full with people grown tired of waiting for the electricity to return. Most of the individuals crowding the stairs seemed to be carrying on conversations with their officemates, or to be simply talking for the giddy camaraderie of something unusual breaking up their Friday routine.

No one seemed to be fleeing from terrorists, though—at least that was a reassurance. Around and around they all went, until finally, after what seemed like long hours, the stairwell finally twisted four times below the second floor and ended at a pair of open metal doors flooded by the emergency lights. Beyond the opening, in the building's spacious marble lobby, resonated the loud voices of a crowd. Soon she'd be in daylight once more.

Relief made her almost push past the gaggle of businesswomen immediately ahead to race for the exit. Now all she would need was to catch a train and be safely on her way home. When her father's shift at the air field was over, he would come home to find Kaylee watching television in her room, his ATM card safely tucked away in his top drawer. Not a thing would be out of place—every item would be orderly and disciplined, just the way he preferred. He'd never have to know how badly she'd gone wrong that day.

Kaylee nearly stopped in her tracks when she reached the lobby and turned her head. Only the crowd behind her, pushing forward impatiently, kept her in motion. There was daylight, true, and an almost deafening hubbub from the hundreds who lined the lobby's every available bench and ledge. They all stared outside, pointing and talking. Mr. Cloutier whizzed right by, making a beeline for the exit as he looked with worry at his watch.

Beyond the glass walls with their open doors, the

streets were crowded with people—seemingly more people than Kaylee had ever seen at one time. They occupied every square inch of the sidewalk, it seemed, standing in the noontime sun, looking around, chattering. What were they waiting for?

How she'd missed it at first she didn't know, but over the heads of the crowd lay a street full of cars, trucks, and cabs, all frozen like a winter river. Horns honked and loud voices argued over the mass of hot steel, a sickly yellow headache of noise and confusion. The traffic lights were out, Kaylee realized as she looked at the intersections where rivers of traffic converged. Every vehicle was at an utter standstill.

So the blackout wasn't confined to this building. For as far as her eye could see, the city seethed with people trying to make their way through streets blocked by unmoving cars. How far did the chaos stretch? For a mile? To Brooklyn?

To Cleveland or beyond?

She somehow was going to have to make her way home in that mess. Sick to her stomach from the sun's glare, Kaylee turned to find Ramon behind her. "What am I going to do now?" she moaned to him.

Ramon's eyebrows raised. He punched a fist into his hand. "Oh, yeah, I knew it! That look on your face? *Money!*" When she didn't comprehend, he explained, "An iceberg. That's what I am. Remember?"

Kaylee loathed his superior smile.

12:18 P.M.

Against Kaylee's skin, the afternoon's heat scorched like a hot iron. The building's lobby had still retained some of its air-conditioned coolness, but the sidewalks had baked in the sun all morning. Their heat seemed to force Kaylee backward against the building's glass doors. It hadn't been this hot an hour ago, when she'd entered the building.

Most of the people crowding the sidewalks seemed almost like lost little kids in grown-up business suits. They wandered around without aim, clutching their briefcases or shoulder bags, jabbing buttons on their cell phones and holding them experimentally to their ears. "Let's get a cab and get the hell out of here," one man with rolled shirtsleeves suggested.

"Where's a cab going to go?" said his friend, gesturing toward the honking, unmoving cars. "With this gridlock?"

The city's streets held a jigsaw puzzle of cars, secured together in a way that Kaylee couldn't imagine ever being taken apart. Funny—the sight was the kind of thing that showed up on the nightly news from time to time, but chaos wasn't what you expected to see twenty feet away from where you stood. "Crazy!" Ramon stood right at her shoulder, leaning in to speak so that he could be heard over the babble of confused voices. "This is a *mess.*"

His finger pointed to the intersection, where a column of steam rose from an old red junker. Somehow the car had jumped the curb and sat with its two front wheels inches away from a deli storefront. Its rusted hood had popped open to canopy a column of radiator steam. A taxi had nearly careened into its side, stopping the traffic in all directions. The store's owner, apron hanging around his fat belly, appeared to be arguing with the car's owner and anyone else in the immediate vicinity. And that wasn't the only argument going on, nor the only accident. Everywhere she looked, someone was standing up from the door of his vehicle or poking his chest up through the sunroof, trying to find a clear route. Kaylee stared at the chaos in utter disbelief, her senses overloaded with smells and sounds and too bright colors.

Was it silly to think she was being punished? If there was some kind of all-seeing eye in the sky, He or She wouldn't penalize an entire city just because *she* had skipped school, right? Ever since she'd woken up that morning, it seemed as if cosmic forces had conspired to make her day absolutely miserable. And it was barely past noon! "Why are you following me around? I thought you were being an iceberg," she growled at Ramon, thoroughly miserable. She didn't like him standing and stretching so close. With his ratty Converse sneakers and his grubby clothing, Ramon looked as if he should smell. Yet he didn't. Although not flowery, like the honeysuckle Kaylee's brain associated with the sound of his voice, Ramon's exposed armpit had its own odor: the spiciness of autumn leaves, mixed with the vaguest remnants of deodorant.

"Even icebergs gotta move," Ramon said. "Haven't you heard of the Ice Age, when all the glaciers came down and rearranged the rocks and stuff? You think they got here by U-Haul?"

"Yes, I've heard of the Ice Age." Honestly—she didn't need a geology lecture from someone who probably rode the short bus to school. "I'm surprised you have."

"I ain't stupid," he protested.

"Fine," she said. "You keep moving like an iceberg or a glacier or whatever, then. Away from me. I'll stay right here."

Why had she tempted fate with those words? At that moment a fresh cascade of escapees from the building pushed them both forward, forcing them into the people ahead of them. "Excuse *me,*" crabbed an older woman, her lips pursed into a sour expression after Ramon elbowed her spine.

"No worries." Ramon smiled.

The crowds, the noise, the heat—it was all too much. Everything seemed to vibrate with a bright yellow sheen, making it difficult to keep her eyes open. She closed them and listened to some of the new arrivals mobbing the street. "I heard on my portable radio that Midtown's the worst of it," said a deep baritone behind her. "Lights are out everywhere, but there's a buncha accidents in this area that clogged everything up."

"Coke truck overturned on Ninth Avenue, I heard," said another woman.

The first man spoke again. "On the radio they were saying they had reports the blackout was reaching all the way to Upstate."

Upstairs in the dark, it had been difficult to believe in a blackout that reached across several states. Faced with all the evidence, though, Kaylee had to admit it might be real. "Cleveland." The word came out of Kaylee's mouth unexpectedly. "All the way to Cleveland."

When she opened her eyes, she found a crowd of people all staring at her in disbelief. *"Cleveland?"* The woman of the overturned truck report had a sharp face and a nose that could cut glass. "What do you know? What have you heard?"

A strained note colored the woman's voice that Kaylee hadn't detected before. "Upstairs . . . "

"She's from out of town." Ramon's hands on her shoulders carried the soft blue of a spring sky, but Kaylee resented it as much as she had Carl's blood-colored grip. What was *with* boys? Why did they always want to grab on and control you like some kind of puppet? "She's from Cleveland," he added, pulling her away. "She wants to get back home. Right?"

"No, that's *not* right. I'm from Brooklyn!" Kaylee growled back as he steered her from the little clump of gawkers. "What the heck?" she demanded, holding up a hand to shield her eyes. He'd moved her out of the shade and into the sun, closer to the curb. The temperature seemed to soar another twenty degrees, straight into the triple digits.

Ramon faced her now, his dark eyes blazing. "You don't go announcin' stuff like that in a big crowd!"

"But it's the truth."

"Don't tell me you never heard of riots." When she didn't respond, he added, "This is New York City. You want to keep out of trouble, you gotta keep everybody happy."

"What's this keeping-people-happy business? You said it upstairs, too."

"It's like my mama always said, you get more flies with honey than vinegar. Keep people happy and they'll give you what you want. Like with that secretary lady."

"The one you flirted with, you mean?"

Ramon shook his head. "Nah. I was just bein' nice, and she was nice back. But out here in the street, people get set off by little stuff, *chica.* Say the wrong thing and you got a situation. That's why you don't start spreadin' rumors."

The fact that he sounded exactly like her father at his most military made Kaylee's teeth ache. "I know what I'm doing."

"How long you lived here?" Ramon challenged. "And don't feed me lines, 'cause I know it ain't been long."

There was no way he could be so certain. Was there? Kaylee tilted up the tip of her nose. "A while."

"Three months? Six months?" They had moved to Brooklyn exactly six cursed months before. Something in her face must have reflected how close he'd come

31

to guessing, because he turned triumphant. "Hah! Thought so. You don't know what happens to city people on a hot summer day. Don't take much to set them off, and then *bam!*" Ramon's sudden yell and the force with which he punched his fist into his hand made Kaylee—and several other people in the immediate vicinity—jump. "You got people throwin' stuff through windows and lootin' and there's cops and tear gas and freaks goin' nuts all over the place. You don't want that, do you? Well, do you?"

"But these people are . . . " Kaylee stopped in midsentence. Another wave of workers exiting the building pushed them farther toward the street. By now they were almost to the corner. She scanned the crowd. "These aren't the kind of people who'd loot. They're . . . "

"White?"

The word felt like a slap across her face. "That's not what I meant. It's not even true." The people standing around them were a mix of all races . . . but admittedly, a larger portion of the men and women tinkering with their cell phones or hauling their laptop bags were fair-skinned, like Kaylee herself. Why did she feel so guilty at his accusation?

"Rich?"

"No! Riots are caused by people like . . . " Why did she argue with the boy? She'd only meant to say that breaking laws was the kind of thing that other people did. By the hostility in his eyes, though, she realized how offensive she'd been. Who was the one person besides herself who stood out in the sea of business suits and skirts? The Latino in dirty street gear, that's who. Kaylee couldn't have insulted him any more if she'd flat out said, *people like you.*

"If you think that rich white folks don't go crazy when the going gets tough, you sure don't get out much." He sounded disgusted, and rightly so, thought Kaylee. Once again she'd opened her mouth before putting any thought behind her words. "You know . . . "

"If I want a lecture, I can get it at home, thanks." The heat was affecting her. That—and the stress—had to be the explanation for her snappish behavior.

"Fine, army princess. Just forget it." It was a dismissal, but also an opportunity. She'd insulted Ramon to the point that he was done with her. She could walk away right then and be free of his irritating, snooping company. For good!

Could she, though? If it hadn't been for Ramon, she'd still be stuck on that elevator. Wasn't it ungrateful, practically accusing him of being a looter? He was probably a perfectly nice guy. An annoying guy who couldn't keep his nose out of her business, but a nice guy all the same. Besides, a guilty voice reminded her, wasn't she the one who'd nearly let Annabelle talk her into stealing money from her dad's bank account? She'd been about to commit a whopper of a crime, and here she was, pretending like she could give lectures about who was good and bad. God! If she walked away now, could she be any more hypocritical? The insight reddened her face.

What felt worse, though, was the recognition that if she walked away right now, she could live with it.

The subway had to be somewhere near, right? She

started to shoulder her way between two much taller men to cross the street. The scratchy fabric of their suits scraped against her arms, first forward, then suddenly back when she found herself being jerked by the arm. "What the—!"

Ramon released her wrist the moment they were close once again, leaving faint prints the color of watermelon on her skin. "Where're you going?"

"Home." When he seemed not to comprehend the word, she added, *"A mi casa?"*

A smile cracked his frustrated face. "Man, your accent is *terrible.*"

She should never have felt a moment's guilt over him. "Fine, catch the accent on this one: *adiós!*"

"You can't go anywhere," he chided.

"It's a free country."

"How're you gonna get back to Brooklyn from here? How? Huh?"

Chills swept over Kaylee's neck and shoulders. "How do you know I'm from Brooklyn?" she stammered. With millions of people in the city, why was she some kind of psycho magnet? Had he been shadowing her all morning? Was he an undercover—what were they called?—truant officer? Could he be one of Carl's friends?

"I'm not sure what planet you were on at the time," he replied. "But you kinda said so when I tried to tell those people you were from Cleveland. *How do you know my name? How do you know I'm from Brooklyn?* You got a short memory, that's how come. I told you I'm no stalker, remember?"

Relief washed over her, but her own stupidity made

Kaylee angry. "Don't get any ideas about following me there, got it?"

"Okee-doke," he said. "But you're gonna be in for a surprise, 'cause I'm from Brooklyn, too." He crossed his arms and squinted through the sunlight at her. "You ain't got a clue how to find your way around, do you?"

"I'm an army princess, remember? We've all got mad survival skills. I've been doing obstacle courses since I could walk. So . . . later." When he didn't reply, she bobbed her head. Hah! She'd told him. "Good-bye."

" 'Bye."

"I'm going!"

"Okay," he said amiably.

Fine. Whatever. She turned to the left and took a single step, swerving to avoid a bicyclist trying to weave her way past. "Nuh-uh," she heard Ramon grunt. When she looked back, he shrugged. "Brooklyn's definitely not that way. I'm just sayin', is all."

The pole holding the street signs stood right next to her. Kaylee peered up at them. He had been right: She hadn't a clue where she was. She'd tried to memorize the subway map on her journey in, but in all the confusion and noise, she'd lost track of which streets ran north and south and which crossed east to west. She refused to dignify Ramon's words with a response, though. Instead, she turned in the opposite direction and took another step.

"Nuh-uh," Ramon said again.

She faced him, ready to walk past, then paused. "Or should I bother?" she asked.

"Mmmmm."

His vague reply made her want to throttle him.

"Okay, so which way *is* the subway?" If he was going to criticize every move, the least he could do was be helpful.

He almost laughed. "Oh, it's the *subway* you're lookin' for, then?"

The vivid yellow of the hot sidewalks, combined with the sour-milk taste of all the traffic noise, made Kaylee's head throb. She clutched at her forehead with both hands. "I can't stand here talking in riddles," she announced, loudly enough that everyone in the immediate vicinity for a second ceased their complaining and conversations to look at her. "My head hurts and I can't stick around here in case . . . " She might as well just say it. "Carl gets out of that elevator and finds me. So point me in the direction of the subway so I can go home. *Now,*" she added for emphasis. It amazed her, how much like an army drill sergeant she sounded.

Ramon stretched lazily, his hips jutting to one side, his T-shirt riding up from the tops of his shorts to expose an inch of lean flesh as perfectly brown as his shorts. "I don't know how they do stuff in the other places you lived, but here in the city, the train stations run on electric." He rubbed his fingers together. "Juice. Voltage. The stuff we got *nada* of. That includes Brooklyn. *Comprende?*"

Only barely did she *comprende*. All this time she'd been assuming—provided she could get past the congestion to a station—that she could simply hop on a train for home and escape this mess. Sure, it might have taken longer, with all the people. The idea had never occurred to her that the trains were just as much paralyzed as the rest of the city. "What am I going to do?" Kaylee's skin crawled with blue pulses of terror. The taste of bile and sour vomit tickled at the back of her throat. She was about to have a full-on, genuine, hundred-percent panic attack. "I've got to get home!"

"Hey, calm down," she heard Ramon say, as if from a distance. "It'll be okay!"

It was too late for reassurances. Kaylee wasn't even supposed to *be* here. She was miles and miles away from her parents' apartment! There was water to cross! She didn't have a boat! Or even a map or compass! She hadn't had any breakfast and didn't have any money to buy lunch . . . wait. Her dad's cash card was still tucked in her pocket, its four-digit code long ago memorized from watching both her parents at the teller machine. She could get out a few dollars, and . . .

The ATM wouldn't be working either, she realized. Once again it became difficult to breathe, with the crush of people surrounding them. Her lungs seemed on the point of collapsing from lack of oxygen. She was royally screwed.

In a jolt of panic she turned and threw out her arms, only to bang one with a loud metallic thud against the street post. Kaylee let out a long hiss of suffering; her eyes seemed to see giant purple and red spots that burst like soap bubbles with every fresh throb of pain. "Crap!" she cursed at last, squeezing her left forearm with her right hand. She'd broken it. The tibia or femur, or whatever the hell she hadn't learned the name of in biology last semester, was probably splintered into a thousand pieces and marrow would leak into her bloodstream and she would die of agony right there in the street and no one would care and no ambulance would come. She was going to spend the rest of her short life on this earth in total and utter agony, and . . .

"You okay? What'd you do that for?" she heard Ramon say in one ear. What was he, the devil sitting on her shoulder or something? "That was kinda dumb."

She didn't bother unsquinching her eyes. *"Thank you very much for your sympathy, Captain Obvious!"*

"What's wrong, honey?" She heard a voice on her other side and felt a hand on her back. She flinched. Even through a layer of T-shirt fabric, the stranger's touch seemed almost chilly. "Do you need to get home? Maybe I could help out."

Kinder words she hadn't heard in ages. Kaylee opened her eyes so she could thank the angel who'd spoken them . . . and found herself looking up at a middle-aged man, well-dressed and carrying a briefcase. He smiled at her with white teeth that glistened in the sunlight. There was nothing identifiably wrong with his face beyond a few pores the size of pinheads and a number of spidery red veins that gave his eyes a bloodshot appearance. Yet despite the heat, the man's offer made Kaylee shiver. His one touch seemed to suck all the warmth from her body.

"No, thanks," she said, stretching across her lips a smile she didn't feel. "I'll be all right."

"Oh, come on, honey." The man's fingers slipped down from her shoulder blade to the middle of her back. "I've got a car parked a few blocks from here. I can drive you right home. Easy-peasy Japanesey!"

It wasn't merely the man's weird expressions that creeped her out. There was something else about him she didn't trust. Sure, he'd offered exactly what she needed. But under any other circumstance she wouldn't hop into a car with a strange man, especially one who stared at her so unblinkingly. Why should she start now? "I said, no, thanks," she repeated, moving. What was that weird taste in her mouth? She wanted to wipe her tongue on the pavement to get rid of it.

"Hey, hey, sweetie!" he protested when she wriggled away. "It's okay! I'm a good guy! I'm okey-dokey-karaoke!"

"No!" she repeated.

"Buddy, lay off her. She's fine. She's with me," Kaylee heard Ramon say from behind her. "Take a hike."

"No harm meant!" said the man, his baritone rising up to the high tenor range. He raised his free hand in the air and stepped backward through the throng of people. "Just trying to be a good Samaritan. Everything's just peachy-keen." He turned and hurried away.

Although she was relieved to be left alone, Kaylee couldn't help but resent that the man had retreated from Ramon and not her. "I was fine without you," she snapped.

"How's your arm?"

She'd completely forgotten about her injury until Ramon reminded her, actually. She nursed the hurt spot slightly. "All right," she said, looking around. More and more people were coming out of the building they'd just exited. Surely it wouldn't be long before Carl's face loomed above the crowd.

"Make a fist for me," he said. What was he now, some kind of neurologist? She closed her thumb against her palm, then wrapped her fingers around it. "No!" Ramon seemed disgusted. "You don't put your thumb inside! When you pop a guy, you'll break it. You do your fingers like this, your thumb goes here, and . . . "

"Uh, hello, army princess here, remember?" Kaylee stopped his demonstration. "I've done self-defense classes, thanks. Why are you showing me this?"

"So you can pop guys like him, next time!" said Ramon, as if the answer were self-evident. "You haul back, nice and straight . . . "

"I'm not popping anybody one!" Kaylee growled. "I'm not that kind."

"You too hung up on *kinds.*"

Kaylee made an experimental fist. "Maybe I should just pop you."

He laughed. "Okay, so you can take care of yourself. You didn't go with that guy. Even if you could have," Ramon pointed out, more serious. "Why's that?"

Who was he, her camp counselor? She didn't need a lecture on self-protection. "Because he was creepy!"

"Why'd you think he was creepy? Looked okay to me."

"I felt it, okay? He didn't seem right."

"Ah-hah!" Ramon jumped a full foot up into the air. The triumphant expression on his face made him look particularly goofy. "So you *felt* something!" Lord. She instantly knew where he was going with this one. "With your *sixth sense!*"

"I didn't." She had, though. Oh, it hadn't been a

sixth sense or anything like that. The man's voice had left a bitter, oily taste on her tongue, she realized. But Ramon was right—that taste, accompanied by the man's too-yearning expression, his cold hands, and his haste to get her into his car, were all part of what had warned her off him.

"You're thinkin' about it, huh? Startin' to make sense, huh?" Ramon still crowed, thinking he'd scored points in whatever stupid competition he was having in his head. "You believe me now, right?" Why was her stupid medical condition so important to him? "So what did your sixth sense tell you about me?"

"Same thing my ears do," Kaylee retorted. "That you're obnoxious and that you never go away."

"Does it tell you I'm a lovah and not a fightah?" he leered.

"Gross out people much?"

"Does it tell you that all the girls tell me I'm the best kisser they ever . . . "

"Hold on." Kaylee closed her eyes and pressed her fingers to her temples, oblivious to the stream of people pushing by. "My psychic super frequencies tell me that if you keep up that kind of talk, in approximately fifteen seconds you'll receive a crushing knee to the groin. How about that one, huh?" Wild horses wouldn't drag out of her a confession of what sensations his voice really aroused. Why should she trust them? That guy with the car, if he really had one, might have been her one easy chance to get home. And where was she? Stuck in a crowd of thousands with a boy who seemed utterly unaware that there was anyone else in the world besides her. "How am I

41

supposed to get back to Brooklyn now?" she complained, once her eyes were open.

She let loose with a ripe curse that anyone in the military might have known but that apparently surprised Ramon. "Oh, no, you di-in't! *Hostia!*" he exclaimed, laughing. *"Estás cojundo!* If your mama could hear you . . . " When she looked around for some escape, he calmed down, and said something in a murmur too low to hear over the crowd.

"What?" she asked, certain he'd said something loathsome.

To her surprise, he repeated, "I'll get you home." She raised her eyebrows. He seemed to interpret her surprise as distrust. "Seriously. Okay, listen, I'm gettin' the idea you're not totally feelin' me, and that's cool. But you don't know *what* you're doin', so . . . " He spread out his arms, hands cupped, appealing to her. "Give me a chance."

She wanted to let him help her. Badly. "What do you want from me?"

"Want? Not money, nothin' like that. Nothin' else either." He thought for a minute, squinting against the noontime sun. "Okay, okay, how about if I get you home without any trouble and don't put my hands on you or nothin', I get your phone number? Or you let me give you mine? Yeah, you let me give you mine. That way you don't got to call me, if you're not feelin' it either."

The bargain was hard to pass up. "No hands?" she repeated.

He shook his head. "Scout's honor."

Kaylee was pretty sure the three fingers he held up

were the Brownie sign, but she had never been a Boy Scout. Maybe they were one and the same. "How are we going to do it?" she asked. "You don't have a car."

"I know somebody who got one. It'll be okay. You'll—hey, let's start walking." He grabbed Kaylee by the elbow and steered her in one of the directions she'd originally tried walking.

"What?"

"Don't look back," he warned, hustling her through the crowd.

Of course, that was the one command in the world that guaranteed she would look over her shoulder, scanning the teeming crowd for some clue to their sudden flight. Finally she spied a familiar face. In the open doorway among a crowd of people making their exodus from the building stood Carl. By sunlight he looked pale and almost shaken from his experience; long minutes in the dark elevator made him squint his eyes and hold up a palm against the relentless daylight.

There was no way he could have seen her from half a block away, could he? Blinded like that?

"Come *on*," said Ramon, insistent. Once more he pulled at her hand. "I told you not to look back."

Did she have a choice? Kaylee followed, though if she had been asked, she never could have explained why. It had nothing to do with the warmth of his fingers against hers, or how they left the faintest traces of a butterscotch taste on her tongue. There were times Kaylee really hated her freakish brain. "Fine," she said, ducking her head and following.

He called back over his shoulder, "So you're gonna trust me, right? Everybody's happy?"

Kaylee didn't answer. She'd rely on Ramon for now, at least until she found a better option. That was the best she could promise—and likely it wasn't something he'd want to hear. But time was ticking. "Where is this somebody you know?" she wanted to know.

"It's kind of a walk from here, but I got to go there anyway to pick something up," he said. "It won't take long. You up to walkin' a few blocks?"

If he noticed that she hadn't answered his question, at least he didn't say. "What are we picking up?" she asked, aware how suspicious she sounded. His laundry? A sandwich? What in the world could someone like Ramon possibly have to pick up?

"Something." Ramon was being just as evasive as she. "You'll see when we get there. If," he added, stepping into the street so they could cross diagonally between corners, "you come clean about why you're runnin' from that buttface, Carl. I'm doin' you the favor, after all. Right? Right? Okay. Now, walk where I walk and don't let no cars pin you. You lose a leg, I'm not carryin' you around Manhattan. No way I'm *that* desperate for a phone number. I get plenty of those." They dodged around a cab whose driver hung out his window, cursing at them at the top of his lungs for lack of anything better to do. "So?" he said, once the yelling had ceased. "You gonna tell me?"

"Right here?" she asked in surprise. "In the street? You mean now?"

Ramon turned around and took both her hands, to help her over two cars whose bumpers touched. The gesture was something a real gentleman might have done, but he ruined it by opening his mouth again.

"When else you think I meant? Not like we ain't got plenty of time."

Kaylee checked her wristwatch. If only that were true. Second by second, her time was running out.

1:13 P.M.

"Daaaaang, army princess!" Ramon looked sideways at Kaylee. "You might be pretty, but you all kinds of trouble! I didn't think you was that stupid!"

Ramon seemed to be testing her reaction, probably expecting her to be outraged or indignant. The sad truth was that he was right. "I didn't think so either," she admitted.

On the upper Midtown sidewalks, people had swarmed in every possible direction like a frantic colony of ants, slowing only in front of the larger buildings, where confused office workers still poured into the open air. For long blocks it had been difficult to talk. A symphony of car horns had prevented Kaylee from thinking, much less piecing together a story for Ramon. Even if some massive electronic failure had silenced the automobiles, the disharmony of shouting voices and of bewildered conversation alone would have drowned out her thoughts.

Kaylee had found herself battling against her brain, trying to distinguish which sensations she could trust

46

and which she had to discard as byproducts of the synesthesia. The scent of gasoline and the unpleasant film it left on the back of her throat were probably from the cars in the street, some of which the drivers still left idling, as if hoping to be moving along soon. Or was her brain making the petroleum odor more pungent and unpleasant because of the crowd's frightened uncertainty? The headache throbbing at the front of her skull in shades of navy blue made her vision shimmer like the air over a sun-baked road. Yet that was surely from the heat and the stress. And she knew the moisture of her armpits was not from any flawed data in her brain, but simply because her anti-perspirant had gone kerflooey.

But Ramon was right. Befriending Annabelle had been a total mistake from the beginning. "I was totally stupid," she admitted. Once they had escaped from the gridlock of the business district and onto some of the residential streets, it had gotten quiet enough to give Ramon a brief outline of the last six miserable months of her life—how she'd been the odd girl out in school when her family had moved from Nevada to Brooklyn, until the day one of the more popular juniors, Annabelle Roche, sat down next to her in the cafeteria, all smiles and compliments. "I was a nobody who transferred in the middle of the winter semester and she was totally pretty and friendly. I mixed that up with being nice, when I should know it's not the same thing at all."

"Yo, this way," said Ramon, stepping off the curb and into the street. The way he snapped his fingers and expected her to obey annoyed Kaylee. It was as if he assumed she was utterly dependent upon him. Then again, who else could she follow? She didn't know where they were in the city—though in the back of her mind she knew that if need be, she could always abandon Ramon and find a police officer or someone to help. Not that they would, in this confusion. At least Ramon had to go in her direction. Eventually. "So, if you knew she was some kind of skank, why'd you let her suck you in, callin' you up this morning and givin' you that sob story about how her dad was beatin' her up and how she needed you to give her money so she could run away? That's screwed up, man."

There were fewer moving cars on this narrower street. People had stepped out of their houses and talked to each other on the steps and sidewalk. Some called to others through open windows. "I didn't know she was a skank! Not until today, when I went running to help her out and found Carl waiting for me. I didn't know she'd been using me all along. I'd blamed Carl for everything. No one told me Annabelle was as bad as he was. Okay, so there was this one girl, Brynne Hohensee. She had the locker next to mine. After Annabelle started letting me hang out with her and Carl, Brynne asked if I knew what a liar Annabelle was."

"So why didn't you listen?" Ramon leapt onto the opposite curb with the gracefulness of a leopard.

As tacky as she found his T-shirt with the cut-off sleeves, Kaylee bet it kept Ramon's armpits a lot drier than her own. She felt embarrassed at the dark, moist stains developing under her arms. "Well . . . " Why hadn't she listened? When she thought back on all the glances the Westchester students had given her whenever she and Annabelle had walked down the hall together, or the catty little comments some of the girls had made in her presence, everything made sense. Kaylee could see now, after the morning's betrayal, that they had been warning her all along. "I thought she was jealous." The words sounded lame as she spoke them. Jealous of what? Brynne had been plenty popular herself. The kids at Westchester Country Day had all been uniformly pretty and privileged. Much more than Kaylee, who had felt like an oddball the moment her army boots hit the school's marble hallways. "I guess I thought Annabelle was different," Kaylee admitted. "I guess I liked her because . . . she liked me. Or pretended to, anyway."

Any decent human being would have heard her glum tone and sympathized. Ramon, however, laughed. "That's what cons do! They make you feel special to draw you in. You should've listened to that Brynne Hohensee girl! Dang, it's a good thing you're stickin' with me. You'd be eaten alive if you was wanderin' the city on your own, for sure." His laughter made Kaylee curl her upper lip. She *knew* she'd been obtuse. He didn't have to rub it in! "She suckered you, and good. Twice!"

"I didn't realize!" she protested to the boy's back, trying to keep up with his long strides. In the midday sun, without sunglasses, she was having a difficult time raising her head.

"Of course not. That's what makes her slick. But I'm slicker. No one pulls nothin' on *me*." Kaylee didn't answer, too busy putting together the puzzle pieces in a

49

way she hadn't been able to in the elevator ride with Carl. For blond, beautiful Annabelle—cheerleader, teen fashionista, queen bee of her set, girlfriend of a football player—to take an interest in a frizzy-haired nobody like Kaylee had been a miracle she'd been afraid to question. They'd held long phone conversations at night, visited the mall together on weekends, swapped gossip in between classes. So when Annabelle had casually mentioned that her boyfriend Carl was having problems with some of his classes, it was natural for Kaylee to offer to help. How totally taken in she'd been! "Can't you slow the heck down?"

"Don't know about you, but I gots places to go." Ramon did drop the pace a little, Kaylee noticed. "And don't be yellin' at me. I ain't the one who asked you to write papers so their boyfriends could put their names on them!"

Kaylee felt contrary enough to say, "Annabelle never *asked*. It just . . . happened."

"Yeah, she made you *think* she didn't ask, so that if something went down and you all got caught, her nose would be clean. She's a good con. You didn't realize she'd been in on it 'til today, right?" Ramon's insight into the situation was so uncannily accurate, Kaylee realized, that she couldn't help but wonder if he had a little bit of ESPN of his own. "Real slick. A player through and through, but slick about it."

What kind of person was she, really? Kaylee wondered about herself. When Annabelle had phoned that morning, crying and barely coherent and begging Kaylee to give her cash so she could escape her abu-

sive father, Kaylee had thought of herself as a trust-
worthy friend. When she'd dashed out of the house
with her dad's ATM card in hand, cut school, and
hopped onto a subway train to meet Annabelle at the
midtown office building, she thought of herself as
Kaylee the Savior, dependable and brave. She thought
she'd been doing the right thing! Who made up lies
about being beaten by their dads?

Yet when she'd arrived and found not Annabelle
but Carl, lurking in his out-of-town father's office like
a spider waiting for its prey, she'd barely had time to
reevaluate the situation before he'd strong-armed her
onto the elevator, headed for the lobby ATM.

"Shut up," she choked out, close to tears. Kaylee's
world had crashed around her the day Carl had been
caught and, under pressure from the teacher and principal, named her as the one who'd written all his se-
nior papers. Today she was ten times the fool for
falling for another of Annabelle's schemes, and she
felt ashamed for it.

"Just sayin' my mind, army princess."

The way he said *army princess* sounded derogatory.
What in the world did Ramon know about her? Or
about anything, especially friendship? He'd probably
never given a turd about anyone in his entire life. At
heart, he probably wasn't all that different than Carl.
Anything for a phone number or a term paper, right?
"How about a little sympathy? I'm the victim here!"
she said as they squeezed between some battered and
empty newspaper vending machines and stepped into
another street.

"You ain't—" Ramon stopped in mid-sentence. His

body jerked and recoiled when, without warning, a shiny SUV turning the same corner nearly ran them both over. Kaylee collided into the arm Ramon automatically outstretched to keep her from stepping out. The driver was a pale woman with a pulled-back ponytail, obviously lost from trying to avoid the gridlock further downtown. She seemed frightened, perhaps at nearly having killed him. Her right hand shot out to press down the lock.

"Aw, not—!" Ramon abandoned whatever he'd been about to say so he could curse rapidly in Spanish. He made a feint, as if he were about to leap at the vehicle and punch his fist through the window. The woman, her expression panicky, swerved and sped off with a bitter-tasting screech of her tires.

Annoyance was written all over Ramon's face when he turned back around. *"La virgen!* Stupid . . . " He seemed abruptly to remember Kaylee's presence and ran a hand over his eyes and mouth, leaving his face blank and cold. "Come on," he said, guiding them once more back out into the street, in the direction of a fenced-in basketball court and playground.

He had deliberately tried to worry that woman! "Why'd you *do* that?" she wanted to know. "You really scared her!"

"She was scared already. I only did what she thought I was gonna do."

"You totally freaked her out, dude! She wasn't going to hit us. It was an accident," she told him. The words came out sounding like a rebuke. "I don't think she saw us, coming around the corner!"

"For someone with all those extra senses, you sure

don't know how to see what's goin' on right under your nose," he snapped, letting the heel of his hand bang against a blue mailbox. It thudded hollowly at the impact. Ramon marched to the playground entrance. "And you know what? You ain't no victim, either."

"You are incredible," she told him, halting Ramon in mid-swing around the fencepost. He turned to face her through the chain-link diamonds. He'd made her angry and she didn't care if it showed. "You just met me. You've got no right to be passing judgment."

"So it's *okay* for someone to make a judgment call on *me*, but if anyone says anything about your army princess self it's all off-limits and stuff?" Ramon clutched onto the fence as if it was the sole thing supporting him. "You ain't no way right."

When Ramon pushed himself off the fence it vibrated and clattered with noise. He started to cross the playground without her. Kaylee stomped through the enclosure and onto the asphalt after him. "What in the world does this have to do with you?" she demanded. "No one said a word about you."

"You, like, totally freaked her out, like, uh, dude!" From the way he squeezed his face and shoulders, and from the over-enunciated way he spoke every syllable, Kaylee guessed he was attempting an imitation of her. She didn't sound like that! She wasn't so . . . fake. The word *dude* sounded false and inappropriate the way he said it—the way teachers sounded when they tried to use slang. Without warning, he switched back to his normal voice when they came close to some adults sitting around a splintered picnic table. "What's goin' on, man?" he greeted the trio, who were crowded

around a portable stereo. Before Kaylee could make a snappy comeback, he held up a hand and told her, "Chill a sec."

Kaylee once had seen a movie about a bunch of people in outer space who had a little problem with aliens bursting out of their chests. That pretty much summed up how she felt at that moment—an angry something battered against her rib cage, wanting its freedom. Except she wanted her alien to strangle Ramon as it popped out. Chill? Fine! She'd chill. She'd chill to sub-zero temperatures. Kaylee crossed her arms and stepped away from the picnic table where the three guys craned their necks to hear what was coming from the speakers. A bunch of kids played basketball nearby as if nothing out of the ordinary was happening. What right did they have to be so happy?

" 'Sup?" asked Ramon, grinning.

The three dark-skinned guys all seemed to be in their late twenties or early thirties at the most. One of them cradled a basketball in his lap and picked at a long Ben Wallace–style Afro with a yellow plastic pick. "Nuthin', Sparky," said another of the guys, a shirtless black man with his hair braided into 'rows. Did Ramon even know these guys? They looked at him like he was the unknown x in a math equation.

"So what's happenin'?" The lean muscles of Ramon's shoulders rose as he gestured around. "Any news or whatever?"

The man with the Afro merely looked up at him and continued pulling the pick through his hair without a word. The third guy, a lighter-skinned man with dirty shorts and gleaming white basketball shoes, said, "Lot of people without juice today."

"Oh, yeah?" said Ramon, casual as ever. "Like how many?"

"All of New York," he said. "Now they're saying Boston. Buffalo. Toronto. Pittsburgh. Cleveland. Detroit." Each city he named left a small static shock against Kaylee's skin. "Everybody."

"So, why'd it go out? They sayin'?"

"Whole lot of white people using their damn air conditioners," said the shirtless guy. Was he looking at her? Kaylee hadn't been using her air conditioner, thank you very much! Although, she supposed with a guilty feeling, it probably was still running at home, where no one was around to enjoy it. Or had been, past tense.

"Sounds pretty deep," was all Ramon could say.

"Yeah, they won't be getting the lights on anytime soon, that's for sure."

"Cool, cool. Aiiiight, y'all. Later."

The men grunted, nothing more. "Yeah, later," said Kaylee, trying to sound as careless as her companion. They stared. Ramon jerked at her hand, glaring at her. They started walking toward the far side of the playground. Kaylee felt their triple scrutiny on the back of her neck.

"Y'know, you could let me do all the talkin'."

"You do nothing *but* talk," she pointed out. Ramon didn't protest when she reclaimed her hand. "And you were rude to me. I don't sound like—like that terrible imitation you did." They were at the far end of the basketball court by now, away from where the kids were playing. Ramon shrugged, jumped into the air, and tried to bang his hands on the hoop's rim. If she had *any* idea of where she was, she would have walked away right then. She didn't. So she tried to make peace, although it was coming out of her mouth in a touchy kind of way. "I didn't make any judgment calls on you." When Ramon turned around and rolled his eyes, she had to modulate her voice to keep from yelling, "I didn't!"

"You didn't. That woman in her fancy Escalade did."

"Wha—?"

Ramon grabbed the pole and pivoted around under the rusty basketball hoop until he once more faced Kaylee. "You saw her." He mimed steering a wheel with his left hand and reaching over his shoulder with his right. "Ka-pow," he said, slapping a spot above his biceps. "Like that. That's all it took. Ka-*pow*."

"I don't get it."

"She locked her door, princess." Ramon looked at her like she was a dim-wit. "A fancy lady drives into a neighborhood she don't know, and what's the first thing she does when she sees a brother of color? She locks the door." Kaylee shifted uncomfortably. "She would've driven all the way home to the suburbs with that door unlocked on a normal day, but when she gets a look at me, all she sees is the shade of my skin."

Is that what he thought of her—that all Kaylee saw when she looked at him was his skin? She could dislike him on any number of other factors, thank you very much. "So that's what this is all about? You're a bigger

victim than me because one random person coinciden-
tally locked her door in front of you and you've decided it's all because of your skin color?"

He crossed his arms, tilted his head to the side, and
stared at her. "You don't got a clue what it's like,
pri . . . "

"Don't call me *princess,*" she warned him, curling
her fingers into a solid fist. He'd approve of that fist, all
right. "Or I'll seriously pop you."

For a split second it seemed as if she'd crossed a
line. Then he grinned, showing a row of white, even
teeth. "Yeah, you'll hit me? All right there, army
princess! You've got some *cojones* after all. Come
on." Once more they were on the move, sidling past a
metal jungle gym and exiting the playground on the
far side, where a rusted and neglected sign warned no
one in particular that all children must be accompanied by a parent or guardian. Kaylee's teeth ground at
the fact that he'd ignored her threat, but it was nothing compared to the irritation she felt when he added,
"And it ain't about bein' a bigger victim at all. Nothin'
I can do about my race or color, so I'm the real victim
here. You," he said, letting Kaylee catch up with him
as they emerged onto a street lined with dilapidated
businesses, "you ain't a victim at all."

After all she'd been through that morning, not to
mention all she'd told him about how she'd been expelled, that was his conclusion? She waited to reply
until they were past an old man pulling a grimy metal
fence over the front of his barbershop. Not, from the
look of the inside, that there was anything worth

stealing inside its ancient interior. "You've got a lot of nerve," she growled at him. "I've been through a *lot.*"

"You might have been through a lot, but you're no victim. You volunteered for that stuff," he said. "You stepped right up with blinders on, signed on the dotted line, and said, *gimme a plateful of what you got there.*" Kaylee felt her face turn red. She wanted to tell him exactly where he could take his accusation and stuff it. And yet, hadn't she been thinking the same about herself earlier? It might have been difficult to say no to Annabelle, or to Carl. Really difficult, in fact. Yet she should have. "You bent over and took it, and then when you got that phone call today you went runnin' for more of the same. That ain't bein' no *victim.* That's just being *stu*—"

Her anger pulsed slowly, the hard, brittle red of a ladybug's shell. Most of it, though, was directed at herself. "Yeah, I get the point, thanks very much." Kaylee felt tired. How many blocks had they walked? Dozens? Three heavy old women in plastic lawn chairs sat on the sidewalk under a hand-painted sign that read MARCIES FASHION'S. Kaylee's English teacher, she felt sure, would have had a fit. Each of them had dark skin covered with red-brown age spots, graying hair, and a paper fan in her hand. They stared without a word at Ramon and Kaylee as they walked by. "When I met you, I was figuring out how to get away from Carl, okay? I wasn't going to take it, that time."

"That's good," he said. "Rule number one: you gotta look out for yourself."

"Where are we, anyhow?" she wanted to know. Try

as she might, she couldn't shake the feeling that she was still the more injured party. Kaylee tried to shuffle aside her hurt and look around for a familiar landmark. A skyscraper, a statue, a street sign, or anything that might clue her in to her whereabouts. Every instinct told her she should always know where she was, in case . . . In case what?

Just in case, was all.

"Almost there." Ramon seemed to know exactly where he was going.

How did he navigate all these city blocks that looked exactly the same? Kaylee wanted something to drink. She wanted a hamburger. She wanted to be home. "Where is *there?*"

They turned another corner, walking from one little street of grubby storefronts and flats to another where elderly black and *latino* men and women shuffled and sat on chairs and steps, and where kids shouted and ran up and down the sidewalk in their bare feet. Every window seemed to be open. "You'll see," Ramon promised.

A red sports car turned onto the street as they came around the corner. Its driver, a middle-aged white guy with thinning hair and wire-rimmed glasses, peered at the street signs as if trying to get his bearings, and then at the various people lining the sidewalks. A glimpse of sunlight caught the ring finger of his left hand as it shot forward. To Kaylee's horror, the man activated his car's power locks.

Ramon turned to her. He said nothing. He merely raised his eyebrows.

Kaylee felt embarrassed. Not only for the man—for herself, and for not fully believing Ramon. "Yeah, I saw it," she said grudgingly, in answer to his unspoken question.

In her head, though, she added, *But I'm not like that.*

1:51 P.M.

The one good thing about having moved to the city, Kaylee thought to herself, was that she only rarely had to go on her dad's Saturday nature outings. Kaylee considered Saturday an ideal day to sleep late, read a little after waking up, and then watch silly cartoons on the television in her PJs while eating massive bowls of sugar cereal. Her father had always been one of those early-to-bed, early-to-rise types, a hearty, barrel-chested outdoorsman who thought Saturday morning meant a granola bar choked down with water from a canteen while sludging through Tidewater swamps, hiking the Chisos, running a desert obstacle course, or trekking through endless Michigan forests. "It's good for you!" he used to bark back over his broad shoulder at her. "Builds character, one challenge at a time!"

Nearly ten years of Saturday hikes multiplied by mile after mile walked in the rain, snow, cold, and heat of all four seasons, and Kaylee ought to have more character than just about anybody by now, by her own calculations. Yet she didn't even have as much as one of her dad's scratchy, rock-hard bricks of granola. Which she really could have used right then, come to think of it. She wouldn't admit her increasing hunger, though, not to Ramon. It would sound too much like whining. If there was anything she'd learned from her dad's pre-dawn treks through the wilderness other than where to put your foot to avoid puddles, it was that whining got you nowhere fast. So she kept her mouth shut and her eyes open, memorizing little landmarks that might help her find her way back, if something happened. In this neighborhood, she hesitated to imagine what could go wrong.

She didn't know that such sections of the city existed, where long-demolished buildings had been bulldozed and weeds had grown up to form stretches of wilderness. Although on either side there were crumbly old brick walls, the narrow field felt like a stretch of prairie picked up out of the countryside and plunked down in the middle of urban blight. Of course, the real prairie might have the same shoulder-high grasses she fought in Ramon's wake, but she doubted they'd be littered with smashed McDonald's boxes, broken beer bottles, and small glass vials. After kicking one of the latter so that it tinkled against a rock, she called out, "Exactly where are we going?"

"Almost there," she heard. "Come on."

The neighborhood's poverty had been bad enough. The debris scattered across this stretch of wilderness activated every warning system she'd been raised with since birth. "No." Kaylee halted. It took a moment for Ramon to double back. "Sorry, but you know, I can't do this any more."

"It's right over there!" Ramon's tone of voice betrayed how much she baffled him. "You can see it!" He pointed in the direction of a gray industrial-looking hulk of concrete looming not fifty feet away. The building's array of paneless windows made it look like a mouth with missing teeth, and the fire escape on its exterior looked as if it were ready to fall into scrap metal on the ground. Somehow the sight didn't inspire Kaylee's confidence. *That* was their destination?

She wasn't having any of it. "Is this some kind of drug deal?" she asked, stating the conclusion she'd begun to draw. Kaylee carefully watched the boy's face. Would she be able to tell if someone like him was lying? Instantly she felt guilty for the thought, and mentally corrected herself. Someone *slick* like Ramon. "Are you dealing drugs? Is that the something you came to pick up?" His head tilted to the side and his eyes opened wide, as if he couldn't believe the words coming out of her mouth. "Don't lie to me, Ramon."

"No!" he protested. "I don't do that sh—dang, girl, what you take me for?"

She still wasn't sure whether or not to believe him. If he was some kind of drug dealer, he wouldn't actually come out and *say* so, would he? On TV shows, a dealer that indiscreet wouldn't last to the commercial break. "Because if you're picking up drugs, I might as well . . . " She let out a four letter word and looked at her watch. It was close to two. Getting home on her own from here would be difficult, but she still had five hours to make it. Maybe she could run into the street and appeal to the scared suburbanites in their SUVs. Of course, with her luck, they'd decide she was some kind of carjacker, call the cops, and she'd land in prison.

"Kaylee," said Ramon. Hearing her name fall softly from his mouth, instead of the more usual *army princess,* surprised her. His lips seemed reluctant to release the syllables. "I ain't pickin' up drugs. I ain't doin' that stuff. It's just a place where somebody lives. Okay? So come on."

That place—that abandoned warehouse or old factory or whatever it was—was someone's home? Was that what he was saying? She couldn't believe it. How could anyone live in a place where the winter winds could swoop in, not to mention the rain and snow and who knew what kind of birds and rats? "Okay. What *are* you picking up?"

"Like I told you, you'll see."

The answer didn't make her feel any better.

They ducked under the branches of a sumac grown wild, crossed through some rubble and over a smashed metal garbage pail, and stepped onto a plateau of concrete whose cracks were thick with weeds. Two corrugated metal doors, once white but now copper and gray with corrosion, blocked what probably used to be some kind of truck loading zone. A chain looped around their handles, fastened by an enormous padlock. In faint blue paint over the way in, Kaylee could barely make out the letters, *S TH CEM NT WORKS.* "You can get inside like—"

"I'm not going in there!" Kaylee was a little surprised at how passionately the words came out, but once she'd said it, she felt more determined than ever.

"You gotta," said the boy, not seeming to understand.

"I am *not* going into some dark . . . disgusting . . . off-limits . . . *warehouse* with someone I don't know!" she practically shouted.

"It's a cement factory," he pointed out.

"Whatever!" Like that one little detail would sway her? "Ramon, this is like one of those bad videos they show in girl's health class where the chick goes to some rave with a bunch of guys and everything ends with ambulances and flashing lights and *Do Not Cross* police tape. What are you picking up? If it's not drugs, what is it? Is it a gun? Some other kind of weapon? A bomb? You don't come to a warehouse—cement factory, whatever—to pick up a takeout order of onion rings and a strawberry milkshake!"

"It's nothin' bad!" he assured her. "Honest. I ain't gonna hurt you or nothin'! If you come in, you'll see. . . . "

"I'm not going in!" she declared, crossing her arms. "You go on ahead. Pick up whatever it is that you can't tell me about that isn't harmless at all and then let's get the hell *out* of here."

"No way I'm gonna leave you out here by yourself!" he said with just as much determination. "That ain't right. What if something happens while I'm gone?"

Was Ramon concerned for her? Really? She felt disarmed. He had a point. At least on the streets, in front of all the crowds of people seeking fresh air in front of their homes, if Ramon tried any funny business, she could have called for help. Dense sumac branches surrounded this particular little alcove; anything could happen to her here, and no one on the streets would ever see or hear. But it didn't matter. She wasn't going into that warehouse. She'd decided that much. "I don't know," she said at last. "I don't know what to do."

What she did know was that she wouldn't give in. Inside her own head, Kaylee carried a long checklist of Things That Are Dangerous that she'd been accumulating since birth. It started with simple stuff—*Don't talk to strangers! Don't touch the stove! Don't play with matches!* Then it moved into more complex propositions, like, *A lot of the nicest boys are only after one thing, so until you know them well, be on guard.* Or the one she should have learned from Annabelle, *If someone's hanging around with the wrong crowd, you can best bet they're probably doing some of the same wrong things.* By dragging her to a deserted, sealed factory to pick up some mystery parcel, Ramon had managed to tick off multiple items on that list. Yet he seemed . . . maddening as it was to admit . . . *harmless.* Annoying, yes. Womanizing, flirtatious, egotistical? Yes, yes, and yes. Dangerous? Every sense she possessed told her Ramon wasn't dangerous at all.

Maybe those more complex items on her internal danger list weren't so different from the ones she'd first learned. Hadn't all the parental lectures Kaylee had heard from birth amounted to the same thing? *Be safe. Don't get burned.*

"Okay," said Ramon at last. "I got an idea. You gotta listen to all of it, though, before you start complainin'. You swear?" Not the most promising start, to be sure, but Kaylee crossed her arms and kept quiet. "You swear?" he asked again. She nodded, to get it over with. "All right, you see that fire escape?"

"Oh, no!" She clapped a hand over her mouth, but it was too late. The protest had already escaped.

Ramon seemed not at all surprised at her outburst. "Dang, funny how I knew you was gonna say that!" He laughed. As color spread across her cheeks, he pointed up to the first landing. "We got to go up to the top. So I'll go inside, climb out a window, and let the ladder down so you can climb on up. You don't got to go inside at all. Yeah?" How in the world could she naysay such a terrible, stupid plan? That fire escape looked so rickety that a good breeze could blow it off the building! Even if they did reach the top, their weight would probably pull its bolts right out of the cement blocks. "It's sturdy," said Ramon in a low, reassuring voice. Had he read her mind? No, probably he'd seen the fear written plainly on her face. "Hey, I wouldn't suggest it if I hadn't done it myself. I come here every week. The fire escape's how I get back down."

"I don't know."

"It's not scary. I mean, dang, if you can hang with that Carl guy, you can climb a fire escape!" His attempt at humor brought a weak smile to her lips. To her nostrils, his promises smelled like orange blossoms, faintly sweet. Why couldn't she have brought nose plugs? "Look, it's the only way you don't got to go inside or be alone long. Best of both worlds, right? I'm not mad at you or nothin'. I'm not gonna make you do anything you don't want. We'll get you home. I'm tryin' . . . "

". . . to keep everybody happy," she finished for him. She knew, she knew. He seemed to mean it. Maybe he and she weren't that different, after all. Wasn't keeping everyone happy the reason she'd practically sold her soul to Annabelle and Carl? She made another face. "Are you sure?"

"Yeah," he said, so soft and sweet the word almost sounded musical. "Are you?"

Ramon seemed so concerned for her feelings that momentarily she lost her urge to argue. The fear was still there, lurching back and forth deep inside the pit of her stomach. Hadn't she learned anything from Annabelle and Carl, the axis of evil? Was she letting herself be talked into some scheme she'd regret later? Somehow, she didn't think so. She had more control here. If the boy turned on her and tried anything . . . well, she knew all the best places to punch and kick: the temples, the Adam's apple, the abdomen, and the ghoolies.

"Wait!" she said, panicking when he stooped down and pulled the corrugated metal back. Surprisingly, it tipped forward, leaving a big enough space to crawl through. "When you're in there we're going to be like, separated," she pointed out, immediately hoping she didn't sound like some big dope. "Not that I need you or anything." He stared at her. Kaylee tried to sound offhanded when she added, "I mean, if you get mugged or hurt or anything I won't know."

"Oh, yeah," Ramon said, nodding. She had a miserable feeling he wasn't buying her bluff. "If I get hurt or something. Okay. Hey, I know." If he realized how very frightened she'd become a moment ago, at the very least he wasn't letting on. "See those windows there?" He pointed at a column of black and gaping panes that extended in regular intervals up the length of the building. "That's the stairs. I can kinda look out while I'm on 'em and you can make sure I'm okay. How's that? 'Cause you never know, I could like, slip and hit my head on something."

She had been listening carefully, but Kaylee couldn't pick out the slightest mockery in his words. Either he was very kind or he was a better actor than she thought. At last she shrugged. Every minute they wasted at this place was a minute they could be using to get back to Brooklyn. "Okay."

Once again Ramon tilted the right padlocked barricade on its hinges. He disappeared through the small, angular entrance it revealed—but not before he poked his head back out and grinned. "It'll be okay, princess. I'll show ya." The metal swung back down with a crash. "Can you hear me?" Kaylee heard him say from inside the building, as if from a long way away. A moment more, and she saw the top of a head briefly appear through a broken pane. "Can you . . . ?" she heard, before it disappeared. Again, the top of the head volleyed up, and back down. " . . . Hear me now?"

She laughed—he was jumping off the floor. He did it twice more farther down the high row of first story windows before finally his face appeared, solid and reassuring, through a cracked square of glass. "Can you hear me now?" he asked again, looking around for her.

Kaylee crossed her arms and tried to sound stern,

but she couldn't help laughing. "Are you trying to sell me a cell phone or something?"

Her reply helped him locate where she'd walked along the building's length. "Oh, cool, there you are. I haven't lost my arm or nothin' yet, see? You okay?"

"Yeah," she assured him.

"Not scared or nothin'? Nah, not you, right?" he added quickly, before she could answer. "Hold on. Just like, twenty more seconds and I'll get there. Okay?" His face disappeared; then a few moments later it poked through yet another jagged gap in the window several feet above. "See? I'm headin' up the stairs. You're doin' good, right? Hold on."

Ramon didn't have to ask how she was doing every ten seconds, but he did anyway. His concern for Kaylee's condition more pleased than irritated her. "I'm holding," she called back to the empty window. Ever since Ramon had entered the cement factory, her skin had felt alive with some sort of sensation—itchy, yes, but not totally irksome. In fact, it was kind of pleasurable, like the height of a blush. Her condition was reacting to some kind of stimulus, but what? Then again, trying to figure out why her synesthesia made her feel certain ways was like trying to find a pattern in the way plastic rodents popped up in the Whack-a-Mole game at a state fair. In the end, it was random.

"I'm here," she finally heard. Near the grated landing above her head, she heard grunting, followed by, "Okay, this ain't gonna work. Hold a sec."

"What's wrong?" she called.

No response. Kaylee stepped back and raised a hand

to shadow her eyes. The upper wooden window frame started to jiggle downward. One moment more and she could see eight wiggling fingers, and soon after that, a head. "Hey," Ramon said, grinning down. "Told you it wasn't gonna be long. Was I right, or was I right?"

He didn't seem to want an answer to that question, luckily. While he squirmed headfirst through the narrow opening at the window's top, Kaylee tried to ignore the squirmy sensation on her skin. What the heck *was* it and why did it have to afflict her now? She smoothed a palm over her arm, trying to rub it away while Ramon struggled to push the frame back into place.

"Okay," he said at last. "Move out the way. I gotta let down the first floor ladder so you can get up. I don't want it crashin' down on your head." Kaylee didn't want that either, but the ladder's descent was surprisingly smooth, considering how rusty it looked. "It's safe," he assured her, jumping up and down in place. "The whole thing's safe. See?" What Kaylee saw were chips of paint showering down in her face, but she tried to pretend it didn't bother her. All she wanted was to get up there with him so she didn't have to be alone on the ground any longer. "Climbing a ladder's easy. All you gotta do . . . "

"I know how to climb a ladder," she told him in no uncertain terms, grabbing hold of a rung so she could haul herself up high enough to grab a foothold. Please! After a lifetime spent on army obstacle courses, she could climb anything. It was mere seconds before she stood beside him on the grating, a story off the ground, not even panting.

"Dang!" Ramon's eyebrows shot into the air. He hauled up the ladder so that no one on the ground could follow them. "I guess so! Come on, monkey girl!"

Kaylee was too pleased with herself to take offense at her new nickname. The fire escape, as Ramon had promised, was sturdier than it looked. Climbing rung by rung from level to level caused the metal's ancient paint to flake away, but underfoot the structure felt solid. At the third floor, below the top story, they paused. Ramon used one of the intact squares of glass to check his hair. "Vain much?" Kaylee asked him, hoping he would realize she was teasing.

"Don't be hatin'. You know you can't resist this," he replied in a lower voice, equally as playful. Then he raised a finger to his lips. What were they shushing for? For a moment, the city was the quietest she'd ever heard, and the sounds began to filter back to her ears—the faintest noises of cars honking in the far distance, overlaid by voices and laughter from the streets closer by. Birds sang in the clump of trees. From somewhere close by came a violin's sweet melody. Kaylee had been so used to the sounds of constant traffic, noise from airplanes in the skies, the raucous, everyday sounds of the radio, and the booming bass of cars blasting music, that the instrument's sweetness caught her off-balance.

Yet the sound wasn't coming from a distance, she realized once Ramon tugged at her elbow to climb the fire escape's last flight. It was drifting down from above, inside the cement factory. Who could be playing so beautifully in such a run-down and disgusting place? It somehow didn't fit.

"Sssssh," said Ramon, once they reached the top. He helped her up to the grating and squatted down, resting his back against the balcony gate and keeping his head low. One of the building's oversized windows sat open there, framing a darkened room inside.

Kaylee also crouched down and peered around the window's edge. "More attention to your bowing, if you please," she heard a deep voice command. "I can tell when you're getting sloppy." At first her eyes only caught glimpses of the walls within—stained concrete and ceilings ruined by leaks. Then she saw motion: the jab and thrust of a violin bow as a small arm moved it to sound out an impossibly fast run of notes. A black man, tall and clad in a patterned black and white tunic, walked behind the player with awkward steps. Dark glasses covered his eyes. With a start, Kaylee realized he was blind. "Nice," he said, speaking to the musician. "Yes, you have been practicing, haven't you?"

Ramon crooked his finger, inviting her to move closer. A smile curved his lips upward as he gazed first at her and then at whomever was playing within. What in the world could have brought out that smile, both so proud and happy? Curiosity made Kaylee lean forward and look through the open window.

The violin's player was a girl—a small girl of no more than nine or ten in a white top and shorts, dark-skinned and dark-haired, nearly as beautiful and angelic as the melody she produced. A music stand stood in front of her, but she played with her eyes closed, leaning into the notes as if they formed a downy pillow that would catch her if she fell. "Excellent. Continue," said the older man. Head erect and nodding to the rhythm, he slowly walked toward the wall until he was out of sight.

How in the world could anyone that young produce something so beautiful? Kaylee had endured a year of cello lessons in the fourth grade and never had produced more than a painful scraping that drove both herself and her parents crazy. This girl played like a professional. Every note sent sweet tastes of vanilla to Kaylee's taste buds.

"Who—?"

Ramon held up his finger to his lips again. Pride shone so plainly from his eyes that it felt almost like an intrusion to look at him, but he leaned forward and whispered, "That's my sister. The one I told you about."

The one born in a mailbag? Kaylee lifted up her head once more to peek over the window's ledge.

She found herself face to face with the blind man, his face menacing and angry enough to fill her mouth with the taste of pepper and dirt. He held a metal baseball bat over his shoulder. "I don't take kindly to intruders," he announced, and hauled back to swing.

2:27 P.M.

"Keeeeee-ryst!" The moment the man's forearms had tensed up, ready to pull back the bat, Ramon had shot out his hands. They now clutched the blind man's shoulders, persuading him not to follow through on the swing. "Hold up, hold up!"

The sound of Ramon's voice was enough to make the man's face transform from angry to wary. His head swung away from Kaylee. "Ramon Xavier Nacio Francisco del Pastor," he said, spitting out the words like grape pits. His voice was deep, husky, and una-mused. "I should bust you upside the head to teach you a lesson."

Ramon let go of the man's shoulders. Once unre-strained, the blind man's arms started to shake. Kaylee realized that they both were as badly scared as she. "Dam—!" Ramon started to say.

"There will be no use of profanity in my abode," proclaimed the man in a voice that still trembled. With a cough, he shook himself so that his brightly pat-terned tunic fell neatly back into place. His fingers

searched for the wall as he spoke, then rested the
baseball bat against it.

"Sorry, George," mumbled Ramon. For the first
time ever, Kaylee thought he seemed cowed. She
swallowed several times in succession, willing away
the spicy taste of fear from her tongue.

After taking a moment to reclaim his dignity, the
older man added, "Where have you been? You're well
over an hour late. And why in the name of all that is
sacred didn't you come in through the front door?"

Ramon pushed his upper body through the open
window, talking rapidly as he pulled himself into the
room. "Okay, okay, hold up," he said. "There's like this
big blackout goin' on, in case you didn't notice."

"No, in fact." The man walked farther back into the
room. Behind him, the little girl was busily tucking her
violin into a case lined with crushed blue plush. "I
can't say I have."

"Oh. Yeah." Ramon added in a stage whisper, to
Kaylee, "He's blind."

"I'm not stupid," she said, not bothering to keep
her voice down. "I can see that!"

"And I'm not deaf." The man reached for the cane
he had left sitting on a chair and leaned onto it. "Who
is your young friend?"

"She's Kaylee. This is George."

In his deep and booming voice, the man intoned,
"Welcome, Kaylee."

"Thanks." She'd crawled into the room while he
talked. The place was a pigsty. No, that wasn't fair. The
mattress in the corner, propped up on wooden crates,
had its sheets made, and the man's few clothes hung

on nails driven into the wall nearby. A stack of over-sized spiral-bound books sat on another crate; the cover of the topmost one was covered with nubbles of Braille. The man had done much to make his place neat and tidy, but the room itself, with its leaks and stains and rubble and its battered door stacked with cement blocks, was decrepit. Well, Kaylee told herself, there's probably not a lot a person could do to make an abandoned factory look like a home. Did anyone know he lived here? Probably not. "I'm Kaylee Gl—"

"Last names are not necessary," said George, raising a hand. "To know mine might eventually prove a liability." With a straight-backed posture and his head held high, he gave the impression of dignity, like a ruler of some far-off nation who'd fallen on hard times. His last comment, though, made Kaylee a little uneasy. Was he in trouble? Or some kind of criminal in hiding?

"Sooooooo. To sum up." Ramon twitched with impatience to finish. "Lights out everywhere. New York, Philly, Cleveland. It's like, totally crazy out there."

"And that is the excuse for your tardiness?" George concluded, turning his head in Kaylee's direction, as if she were the unspoken question mark at the end of the sentence. Ramon stared at her too, and so did his sister, her big brown eyes reading Kaylee's t-shirt, then taking in her pulled-back hair, shorts, and sneakers.

In a lightning round of Which of These Things Is Not Like the Other, Kaylee would already have been ousted as the obvious outsider. With three sets of eyes on her, Kaylee suddenly experienced another twinge of shyness. Was she supposed to say something? "Why didn't you guys notice the blackout?" she asked, before the silence overwhelmed her. "I mean, it's been like, two hours."

George's dark sunglasses gleamed in the window's reflected light. He spread wide his hands. "My abode is naturally electricity-deficient," he explained. "And when one is mastering Marie Lemley's *Concerto for Violin in B minor,* an exquisite work in the hands of a true artist, one's attention tends not to wander to . . . " Ramon had let out a showy yawn for Kaylee's benefit, winking at her during the speech, but somehow George had picked up on it. "Boy, don't make me come over there and smack you."

Ramon's sister had been silent up to this point. With her brown eyes, long, dark hair, and skin the color of creamy coffee, she looked like a living doll—the kind that blinked and cooed and lisped sweet baby talk. For the first time since their arrival, her lips parted to speak. "Smack the *crap* out of him," she urged George. Kaylee's jaw dropped. "Don't be giving me that look, hoochie mama!" she added, glaring at Kaylee. "I know you've been kissin' up on my brother when he was *supposed* to be pickin' me up from my *lesson.*"

"Rosa!" said both George and Ramon simultaneously.

"That kind of talk is not what young ladies . . . "

". . . *not* kissin' on some *gringa flaca* . . . "

". . . when there are many other more appropriate . . . "

". . . you make it sound like I'm always kissin' up on girls when you *know* . . . "

". . . classical music is not merely something that's

played, but a style of *living* that is at once *gracious* and . . . "

The general clamor was already renewing Kaylee's headache. Rosa raised her voice and yelled, "Why you two always tellin' me do this! do that!"

" 'Cause I'm your brother, that's why! Who else is gonna look after you if . . . "

". . . role of a mentor is a very important . . . "

"Stop it!" Every angry word made the fiery veins crossing Kaylee's vision throb. The three-way squabble was like listening to one of her parents' rare fights— stupid words thrown back and forth over senseless things. When Kaylee opened her eyes again and pulled her hands from her ears, she found both Pastors and the music instructor staring at her. "Oh, my God, you're like some kind of weird dysfunctional family! And I already have one of those!"

"Dis-*what?*" Rosa snapped, putting her hands on her hips and marching right up to Kaylee. "Oh, no, you didn't!" She let loose with a mouthful of four-letter words. Kaylee had heard them all before, of course, but coming from the mouth of a munchkin . . . wow. Just—wow.

"Rosa!" Ramon scampered forward and scooped up his sister in his arms, as if trying to keep her from— what? Kicking Kaylee in the kneecaps? She was big enough that he had to lean back to keep her balanced on his hip, but it was obvious from the way her arms went around his neck and her head automatically cuddled on his shoulder that she adored him. Her look of contentment and love was reflected in Ramon's expression. "We're tryin' to teach her to be a *lady.* A real lady *who don't cuss,*" he said with emphasis. Rosa stuck out her tongue. "So she can get into a special school."

"Her performance skills are exemplary. It's obvious that she practices, but . . . "

"She practices! She practices like, all the time!" Ramon assured George.

"I *practice* so I don't have to listen to your fat mouth tellin' me to do all kinds of shi—"

"Rosa!" Kaylee found herself joining in this time.

Rosa looked around at the three older people shouting at her and rolled her eyes. With a wriggle, she scooched loose and went to collect her music and her backpack. "Whatever, peeps. Y'all ain't the ones who had to spend two hours on your feet playing this god-d—" A single raised eyebrow from George quelled whatever obscenity might have come spilling from her lips. Listening to Rosa's potty mouth was as shocking as witnessing the prettiest Christmas angel suddenly spew profanity in the middle of "Silent Night." She faced the group and tossed back her hair. "Who said I *want* to go to a special school, anyway?"

"Child, I don't know how many times the pair of us and even your own sweet mama, God bless her, have been over this with you," said George, turning around to locate the direction of Rosa's voice. "When the good Lord gives you a gift, it's up to you to use it to the fullest. You don't hide your light . . . "

". . . under a bushel, *whatever.* Dang, I don't know what a bushel *is.* I ain't gonna go hidin' no light under it."

"Princesa!" Ramon coasted across the old wooden

floor on the knees of his long shorts until he glided to a stop in front of his sister. "You know you're the best thing that ever came out of this family! *Mami* and me, we're so proud of you we could spit! All we want to do is get you into this school so you can grow up and shine, *princesa,*" he promised. Kaylee itched to speak, but she didn't dare interrupt. Not now. "But you can't get no scholarship if you let the people who are gonna interview you think you're all rough around the edges. You gotta act like a little *lady.* Okay?" When Rosa looked at the floor, not answering, he shook her hands, his voice soft and wheedling. "Okay? C'mon, give it a try. I know you can."

"Oh, all *right.*" Rosa didn't look at all happy about the bargain. "But no dresses."

"You don't have to wear a dress to be a lady, *princesa,*" Ramon cooed. It was sweet, really, how very much he obviously adored his little sister, but Kaylee shouldn't have been surprised. Hadn't one of the very first things she'd learned about him been how special he thought his sister was? "All you've got to do is play your little sonata in—"

"Concerto," corrected Rosa, arms crossed.

"All you've got to do is play your little concerto—"

"Madame Marie Lemley's *Concerto for Violin in B minor* is a *major* work of the late Romantic repertoire," Rosa informed her brother, with a sideway look at George to be sure she was getting the information right. Her teacher gave her an approving nod. "It's not *little.*"

"See, play your piece and wow the panel with that kind of talk and you'll get that scholarship. You want it, I know. Right?" Rosa shrugged at first, but then, after he looked her straight in the eyes, she nodded. "You can do it, baby, I know it. Ain't nobody half as good as you. You're gonna end up big. Hear me?"

Kaylee watched the two embrace for a moment before butting in. It was as good a time as any. At least they both had their mouths closed . . . for a change. "Listen," she said, taking a step forward. "Ramon, I don't want to interrupt or anything, but you promised . . . can we hurry it up?" She looked at her watch. "You said you knew someone with a car, and it's getting later, and I'd be a *lot* happier if we could get going."

Rosa broke away from the embrace and stared as if Kaylee had hocked a gob on her. Ramon blinked once, then twice, and came to from a faraway place. "What?" he asked. "Oh. Oh, yeah. George, your car got gas?"

Before the man could answer, Kaylee said, "Wait a minute. It's *George's* car? Do you drive?" she asked Ramon. She'd noticed that a lot of people in New York didn't, and she certainly didn't know how. Driver's Ed was one of the privileges that had been yanked when she'd been expelled.

He shrugged. "Nah."

Incredulous, she looked from Ramon to George and back again. "I don't care how good a music teacher he is, I don't think that *he* can—"

"The vehicle to which my young friend refers is one that, let us say, found its way into my possession when I took up residence in this fine abode." George gestured with his hands. "Though not glamorous, it is quite serviceable. Unfortunately, at the present time it is in the capable hands of Andre. My son," he added for Kaylee's benefit.

All this fuss, all this bother, all the climbing and walking and all the fear from nearly getting her head bashed in—it had been solely so they could get to this car Ramon had promised. And the car wasn't here. Of all the idiotic, half-baked . . . not even half-baked! Ramon's plan had been raw, unappetizing cookie dough all along, studded with chunks of cement instead of chocolate chips. She could have been a quarter of the way home by now!

Ramon must have seen the fury rising in Kaylee's expression, because once more his voice took on the reassuring tones he used whenever he wanted to keep everyone calm and happy. "Hey, it's okay," he told her. "Andre's at work, right? At the pizza parlor? We can go over there."

"If he's working, I don't think he'll be able to drive us anywhere." Kaylee's words came out snappish, but she didn't care.

"He might!"

Before they could break into an argument, George intervened. "If indeed there is a blackout, I sincerely doubt that any of the pizza-making apparatus is functional," he said. "Ergo, he should be able to drive you where you need."

Kaylee hesitated. At this point she might have a whole boatload of regrets, but she didn't have a better suggestion. "How far away is this pizza place?" she asked, grumpy.

"I don't know, maybe ten blocks?"

Kaylee's ankles ached at the number, but she didn't say a word. How many New York City blocks were in a mile? Twenty, wasn't it? Rosa raised her voice in shrill complaint, however. "I ain't walkin' no ten blocks!" When Ramon's head snapped around, his eyebrows raised, she amended, "I mean, I would *prefer* not to have to *walk* such a lengthy *distance,* if you *please.*" It was like some weird elementary school version of *My Fair Lady.*

"We're gonna have to walk a lot farther if we don't," Ramon told her. "Like all the way back to Brooklyn farther. Get your stuff."

Mumbling to herself, Rosa picked up her violin case and backpack from the floor. "I don't *want* to walk that far."

Kaylee tried to make her feel better. They hadn't, after all, gotten off to a very good start. "Me neither, honey, but it's better than walking all the way back to Brooklyn."

"I ain't your honey and I *definitely* don't want to be walkin' with *you,*" Rosa added, stomping away. Her violin case flailed on its handle as she made her way to the window. The three of them watched as the little girl leaned over the sill, dropped her possessions on the fire escape, and hefted herself over.

In a quiet tone, George asked, "Before the blackout, did you get downtown to talk to—?"

Whatever he'd been about to ask, Ramon cut off with a curt, "Yeah. Let's not talk about it."

"Boy, I've told you a hundred times, you can't spurn—"

"I can spurn what I want." Ramon sounded uncharacteristically gruff. "No offense, but it ain't your business."

"Rosa's future—"

"All I think about is Rosa's future, all right?" Ramon barked back. Then, calming down, he said, "Sorry, George. I know you got a good heart. Stuff with you-know-who is . . . weird."

Kaylee wasn't following any of the conversation; she was too aware of every passing minute and how much time they were losing. Why couldn't Ramon hurry?

"Well?" she heard from behind her. Rosa had stuck her head back through the window, obviously wondering the same thing. "Are we gonna go before I don't *got* a danged future?"

"Rosa!" chided Ramon and George in chorus.

"I mean, may we depart now?" she asked, words drenched with syrup, her cherubic face masking the foul-mouthed little girl behind it.

Kaylee wasn't sure which Rosa alarmed her more.

3:02 P.M.

"I didn't get lunch." Rosa yelled over the pickle-flavored merengue beats of a portable radio on the sidewalk. "I said, I didn't get no lunch." A moment later, "I'm hungry."

The nicest thing about having Rosa around, Kaylee decided, was that she uttered anything that came into her head—and a lot of the things in the girl's head were the very same as in Kaylee's. Her own stomach was convulsing in prickly waves of hunger, occasionally complaining so loudly that it had to be audible over the sounds of people talking in the street, the radios, and the cars passing by that boomed with heavy beats. Rosa was saving her some serious whining time. "I didn't eat either," Ramon told his sister.

"That's because you was too busy kissin' up on your *girlfriend.*" Rosa looked over her shoulder, eyes ablaze.

Was Rosa upset at the mere fact that Ramon had showed up with a girl? Or was she being hateful at Kaylee herself? "I'm not his girlfriend." The dislike could flow both ways if the girl was going to be that obstinate.

"Huh, guess that makes you some kind of cheap—"

"Rosa!" Ramon rattled off some harsh-sounding Spanish. Even when speaking a language Kaylee didn't understand, his voice was still perfumed with sweetness. She still caught whiffs of it now and then, though she'd grown used to its presence. He shook the little hand he held in his own. "Now apologize."

"No."

"I said, apologize!" Ramon sounded more like the girl's father than her brother.

"Fine." Rosa sounded as if it was anything but, yet she turned around and faced Kaylee. "I am *ever so sorry* you're nothing but a cheap—"

"Rosa!"

"You know, Ramon, it's okay. She's cranky. You were late, she's hungry. We're all hungry." Being with someone more crabby than she allowed Kaylee to feel a little gracious. It was like the slight superiority you got from hanging around with a kid who didn't make quite as good grades. Geez, was she vain or what? That was exactly how Carl had managed to sucker her in to his scheme, wasn't it? Appealing to her enormous vanity? She'd felt *good* knowing that of all the smart kids in the school, he and Annabelle had come to her for help. What kind of raving egomaniac did you have to be to fall for flattery and praise? Whatever kind, she was the worst there was.

"Well, if you wasn't kissin' up on your girlfriend, Manuel was probably takin' you out to lunch and buyin' you fancy stuff, so I know you not as hungry as me!"

They walked down the street, back in the direction from which Ramon and Kaylee had originally come, passing the mental landmarks she'd noted earlier. In the middle of the narrow one-way street, a single lane of traffic crawled to the intersection. A block and a half away, Kaylee could see a number of flashing police lights. Was there an accident or something?

If anyone noticed anything unusual about Kaylee tagging along behind the Pastors, they didn't say a word. In fact, no one seemed to notice her at all. The many people crowding the street were all too busy going about their own business and shouting out news of the blackout from group to small group, or talking through open car windows to the people stuck in traffic. Ramon glanced back at Kaylee as she regarded the street and said to Rosa, in a low voice, when he seemed to think Kaylee wasn't listening, "Manuel didn't buy me no lunch."

"Why not?" If Ramon was trying to keep their conversation secret, Rosa wasn't picking up on the cues. "He's got plenty of money."

"Money don't make the world spin, *princesa*," Ramon said, again keeping his voice low.

"Then why are you so hot to get me into this fancy school?"

"That's different."

"How?"

"It just is."

"How?"

"It just *is.*"

"But how?"

"It just . . . "

The conversation was like nails on a chalkboard. The Pastors were driving her nuts. Kaylee couldn't take it anymore. "Who is Manuel?"

"Nobody," said Ramon.

"Our brother," said Rosa at the same time.

"Half." For the first time, there was a faintly sour trace in Ramon's speech, like that of apples left to rot on the ground. "Half brother. It's family stuff, Kaylee, you don't got to be worryin' about . . . "

Though he kept talking, Kaylee didn't hear a word. Her brain had shifted into overdrive, overloading synapses with neurons that fired so rapidly she could barely tell what was real and what was illusion. One moment she had been walking down the street and listening to the Pastors argue, everything normal. Then the next, her everyday vision had been hijacked and replaced with special effects from *The Wizard of Oz*, where everything she saw was dull, Kansas gray—save for one spot of blazing, unmistakable color. In the distance, she recognized a broad-shouldered boy stopping to ask someone a question, his head bobbing and weaving as he spoke. His lips were pressed together, tight with annoyance. The person replying to him obviously hadn't answered in a way he liked.

Carl. What was he *doing* here? Her vision became normal again as suddenly as it had faded to monochrome. Despite the change, Kaylee didn't take her eyes from the danger waiting less than a block away. She knew the answer to her question. Carl had hunted after her, tracking Kaylee and Ramon through the city streets.

Instinct took over. Kaylee scrambled sideways beneath an awning, sheltering herself in the doorway of a corner market. Breathing seemed difficult, suddenly. The temperature had to be at least a hundred degrees. What if she'd kept walking, not paying attention, and run right into him? Would she have even noticed Carl if her brain hadn't gone wonky on her? Screw speculation. None of it mattered at the moment, not with Carl hunting her down like a bloodhound.

Neither Ramon nor Rosa had stopped with her. She hadn't had time to warn them, and now she didn't dare peek her head around the corner of the alcove to see if they were still within shouting distance. Her skin color already made her highly visible in this neighborhood—drawing attention to herself would be stupid. Yet what if Ramon disappeared entirely and never came back? Now that he had his sister, would he even bother to find out why she'd lagged behind? What if he shrugged and wandered away and she never saw him again after everything they'd already been through? Kaylee wasn't sure she could bear the thought. But why?

She couldn't think about Ramon. She had to look out for herself first. Caring about other people who didn't give a damn about her had been what had landed her in this mess to begin with.

While people briskly entered the market and others exited carrying out flats of water bottles and armfuls of bread and other foods, she tried to calm down and consider her options. If the Pastors didn't come back, she could . . . she could hide. Yeah, hide somewhere. Where, though, in a strange neighborhood? Did phones work during a blackout? Yes, of course. Some people's cell phones might have gone haywire, but not all of them. And the Versatekk receptionist had been on a land line after the blackout. Maybe she could call someone. Who? Her dad? And tell him exactly where she was, when she was supposed to be sitting at home in her room by now, doing her homework like a good girl? She had promised her parents to prove that she was worthy of their trust. Running around Harlem with a strange boy on the hottest day of summer didn't qualify. Her dad would send her off to some awful military school for sure, where she wouldn't know a soul and where they didn't let anyone home for Christmas and where she'd have to repeat the whole tenth grade over again! She'd be miserable and weepy all the time, and . . .

"Ow!" Kaylee yelled, when sickly yellow spikes of pain shot from her knee.

She looked down to see Rosa's violin case still swinging. "I *said,* wake up." The little girl's eyes were dark and her mouth was twisted into a scowl. "We walked all the way back here to find your sorry butt!"

Ramon also stood in front of her, real and solid, his mouth twisted and his eyebrows raised. "You're here! I mean, you didn't leave me!" Kaylee said, grabbing his fingers. Despite the throbbing in her knee, she'd never been so relieved in her life.

Without saying anything for a moment, Ramon studied her face, then looked with surprise at her hands clasping his own. "You thought I'd leave you behind?"

Kaylee didn't have time to explain. "Carl," she said. The one word automatically made Ramon's head twist.

She pointed him in the right direction. "No, over there. He's been trailing us."

Several times, Ramon tried to peek out around the alcove's edge, but he was equally as cautious about showing his face as Kaylee had been. "Rosa," he said at last, "do your brother a favor and step out and see if you can spot a goofy-lookin' white guy wearin', uh . . ."

Goofy was a good word for Carl. "A red Polo shirt and Dockers," Kaylee said. From her brief glance, she could tell Carl was already pink from too much sun. It made his skin look even more like a plucked chicken. Rosa looked ready to resist, but when her brother narrowed his eye at her, she sighed, stomped out into the street, and looked around. Kaylee's anxiety seemed to multiply with every passing second.

"I'm too short," Rosa complained, on tiptoe. She looked around and finally walked out to a shabby old Chevrolet stopped in the long line of traffic in the street, put one foot on the bumper, and stepped up onto the trunk so she could peer over the heads of a crowd much taller than she. "Shut up, it ain't like you got a Rolls-Royce or nothing," she told the woman driver, who had stuck her head out the window and begun squawking in protest.

Ramon grinned. "It'll be okay," he reassured her.

When he gave Kaylee's hand a squeeze, she realized their fingers were still interlocked. She flushed a little, embarrassed, but her shyness vanished when Rosa called out, "Oh, there he is. He's got a big head."

"What do you want to do?" Ramon asked, as Rosa

hopped down from the car and made her way back over.

Kaylee shook her head. A man exited the market carrying a box of evaporated milk and several more boxes of sugary breakfast cereal. She watched him stride out onto the sidewalk. "We can't let him see us," she said, stating the obvious.

"We could go through the store, see if they got a back way out, go around him somehow."

"It's a start," said Kaylee.

"Let's try." Still holding tight to Kaylee, Ramon took Rosa with his other hand and led them through the front door of the market.

An apron-clad man stood within, watching who came and left. He merely nodded at the kids, keeping an eagle eye on a few people heading for the exit. "We still got bottled water, if your moms sent you for that. Not much, though. Cash only." Ramon nodded his thanks, and they stepped through a short row of produce, colorful and, even in the city's sweaty center, smelling of the earth.

The store was fairly busy with customers anxious to make purchases. No one, however, was pushing or shoving or complaining much about having to stand in one of the two long checkout lines near the store's entrance, where clerks added up prices on battery-operated calculators and made change from open cash register drawers. The women standing in line fanned themselves with magazines and small hand fans printed with Bible verses. Some boasted curlers in their hair and wore housecoats; others looked as if they were on their way home from office jobs. A few men stood in the lines as well, their chubby fingers clutching the handles of six-packs. Yet all the customers talked to each other as if they had all the time in the world.

Kaylee wished she could stay among that unhurried crowd, where no one seemed to worry about anything more than collecting candles and water for the night ahead. In fact, their little trio seemed to be the only people in the entire market with anything on their minds. "Hey, kids, hold up, not so fast," said another green-aproned clerk when Ramon swung around the refrigerated meats onto the frozen foods aisle.

"You got a back way out?" asked Ramon. It sounded suspicious, the kind of thing bank robbers might say in a movie where they were running from the police. Luckily, he quickly added, "My little sister, she gotta pee *real* bad."

"No, I don . . . !" When her brother gave her a quick shake of the wrist, Rosa glowered. "Yeah, I do. Bad."

The clerk looked over his shoulder at a swinging door beyond the freezers. "Well, there's an alley out back, but . . . don't you want to take her somewhere a little nicer? We've got an employee restroom."

Rosa smiled sweetly at the man as they walked by, using the voice Kaylee recognized as ladylike. "Oh, no, thank you, kind sir, my brother makes me pee in alleys *all* the time. He says I'll be spoiled by indoor plumbing. Thank you *ever* so, though." Even with Carl's proximity stressing her out, Kaylee wanted to snort with laughter.

The clerk called after them, as Ramon led them

94

swiftly toward the back, "Hey, you kids want some ice cream? We've got to give the stuff away before it melts." He held up a gallon of butter almond. "Take a couple? Free?"

"Yes, please!" Rosa's violin case swung in a high arc when she tried to lunge out of her brother's grasp. The case came crashing down to her side as Ramon barreled through the back room door, dragging both Kaylee and Rosa behind him. *"Clavos de Cristo!"* snarled the little girl, once through. A tired-looking stock boy looked up at them in astonishment from a wooden palette where he was taking a break, Mountain Dew bottle half-finished in one hand. The room was cluttered with more empty cardboard cartons than probably should have been there; another boy scarcely any older than either Ramon or Kaylee was pulling plastic bottles of water from storage and loading them onto a trolley. "Are you guys *deaf?* Free ice cream!"

"We'll have a couple of minutes once we get out to the alley. What then?" Ramon asked.

"Free!"

"I don't know," Kaylee told him. She pushed on the outer door with her shoulder until it gave way onto a narrow alley. The rancid smell of the Dumpsters sitting a few feet away made her skin feel clammy all over. "How far away is the pizza place?"

"Ice cream!" shrilled Rosa. *"All we can eat!"*

"Kind of a distance," he said. On both sides of the alley stood tall buildings, the mortar holding together their bricks crumbling and worn with weather and age. A dead-end side street lay a few steps to their right. As bad as the Dumpsters smelled, at least their steel bulk hid the three of them from sight. "How did he find us? Was he askin' people questions?" Kaylee nodded.

"You guys totally reek." Rosa wrenched free her hand. "We could be eating that ice cream right now instead of you two standing around making goo-goo eyes at each other."

"We're not making . . . !" Kaylee suddenly felt very self-conscious that she still held Ramon's hand. She hadn't let go since she'd taken it in front of the market, but she now relaxed and let herself slip away. Ramon's fingers left warm, velvet traces on her wrist and palm that began vanishing too quickly. "Sorry," she said, wondering at the same time why she was apologizing.

"And if I hear the words *ice cream* outta your mouth one more time . . . " Ramon let his threat die. Did he notice their fingers no longer touched? Oh, she was crazy! Her hand was probably one of a thousand for him. Of all the stupid things in the world to be focusing on, holding a strange boy's hand was the least of them.

"You'll what, smooch me to death with your smoochy killer smoocher lips?" Rosa looked so serious that it was a surprise when she dissolved into little-girl giggles and started to run around in shrieking circles. Ramon lumbered after her like Boris Karloff in the *Frankenstein* movies, lips pursed, hands clawing in her direction.

Funny how that commonplace little silliness gave Kaylee a mental foothold. Blackouts that extended who knew how long, betrayals, all the trouble she was already in—they all were too big for her brain to grapple with in an organized way. It was like trying to comprehend the size of the universe, or how long eternity really was. Think about those things too much and she would go totally crazy. But the stupid ways brothers and sisters treated each other . . . that felt totally normal. It was like a plunger to the clogged pipes of her brain. "Okay," she said with sudden decision, "I really think we ought to look for a ride at this point." When Ramon stopped chasing his sister around, she explained. "It's way after three. There's got to be a bus or something. Think about it: The only way Carl could follow us here is because we passed a bazillion people on the street who could tell him they saw a girl with an army princess T-shirt."

"You could take it off," was Ramon's not-so-helpful comment.

"Dream on, you big pervert. I'm trying to be serious here. And it's not like there aren't two dozen people standing in line who didn't see us fly past just now, if he decides to ask inside." A shiver went up Kaylee's spine at the thought. "We need to find someone with a car, and soon, and I don't think it's going to be the pizza parlor guy."

"Why not ask *her?*" Rosa wanted to know. She pointed to a new-model Mercury Grand Marquis idling at the side of the dead end, where a white woman fluffed her dark hair in the rear-view mirror. She and the dark red car looked as much out of place as Kaylee—probably yet another lost commuter.

"You can't walk up to someone and ask . . . "

Kaylee, however, had forgotten what kind of ten-year-old she was dealing with. Barely were the words out of her mouth than Rosa had already approached the car, violin case clutched to her chest. She rapped on the window.

"Rosa!" Ramon sounded more annoyed than angry. Both he and Kaylee followed.

The little girl ignored them both, rapping on the passenger side window again. When the woman reached across the car, for a moment Kaylee felt certain she was going to push down the door's lock. Instead, she fumbled for a moment at the controls until at last the window whirred halfway down. "What?" she asked in a deep voice. The eyes that peered over the tops of her oversized sunglasses were bloodshot. Obviously she was older than Kaylee had first thought: probably in her early thirties.

"Hi, lady!" Rosa spoke in her sweet voice, cuddling her violin while she pivoted from side to side. If Kaylee hadn't known what a little demon child lurked underneath, she would have been charmed herself. "Are you lost, ma'am?"

For an impossibly long moment, the woman looked over her shades at Rosa and then at Kaylee and Ramon. Her jaw worked up and down, grinding a wad of chewing gum. For a relatively pretty woman, she was dressed in drab colors that almost seemed to make her fade into the car's tan interior. "Why?" she said at last.

"Because my Sunday school teacher says that when good Christian people are in trouble, they should help each other out!" Did people really say *ay yi yi!?* Kaylee wondered. Because that's exactly what it sounded as if Ramon muttered under his breath. Kaylee felt torn between stopping Rosa from embarrassing them all and cheering her on. "And we're looking for a ride, and if you're lost, well! We could help each other!" The woman looked skeptical. Rosa quickly added, "Like Jesus said."

Before they lost the woman completely, Kaylee bent down and looked through the window. "We need to head a little ways downtown. If you're not going far, even a few blocks would be a help."

"And I know how to get anywhere," Ramon chimed in. "I can help out if you're lost or if we got to miss the traffic jams."

"I'm carrying a violin," Rosa said, hefting up the case. "In case you didn't notice. It's heavy."

"You don't have a machine gun in there, do you?" the woman asked. Her voice had a peculiar scent to it—like some sort of wild, peppery weed, Kaylee thought. "Joke. Kidding. Yeah, you know," she said finally, nodding, "you kids actually might be a big help. Get in. You get in the front, hon," she told Rosa.

Kaylee had never heard sweeter words in her life, though they felt like a kick in the head. Could finding help really have been that easy, all along? "God bless you, nice lady," said Rosa, sweeter than three pounds of cake frosting with sugar sprinkled on top. Either the kid needed to cut it out or stop laying it on so thick.

Against Kaylee's back, the leather seats felt like ice. "Air conditioning!" she exclaimed, basking in the blast of frosty air blowing at her between the front seats.

It was amazing how fantastic a cold gust could feel. Ramon opened his mouth to gulp in the coolness as if it was water and he was parched. Soon the two of them were competing for the breeze. "Put on your seat belt," he said over the seat.

"Oh," said the woman, grasping around to find the buckle. "Okay." Kaylee and Ramon looked at each other and blinked, surprised.

"He meant me," Rosa told her, already snapping shut the latch. "What's on your CD player?"

"Oh." Was something seriously wrong with the woman? Why was she so vague about everything? Kaylee's nose still tingled with the peppery scent, causing her to sniffle. "You know, little girl, I'm not sure." Kaylee watched as the woman's fingers groped at the expensive-looking car stereo on the console.

"Don't you know how to work it?" Rosa asked.

"New car. I'm not used to it yet. Why don't you look and see?" she said at last, putting the Grand Marquis in gear and pushing up her sunglasses so they sat squarely on the bridge of her nose.

"Where is it you're tryin' to go?" Ramon still leaned over the seat, but contorted his body to let Kaylee have her half of the air conditioning.

The woman was too busy searching for something in the visors to answer immediately. After a moment, she gave up. "Let's see what happens after we get through the police block."

"Police block!" Kaylee exclaimed. It sounded dire.

"Yeah, didn't you see it when we were on the street?" Ramon asked her. "All the lights and stuff?" She had, but she hadn't known what it was. "Sometimes they set up police blocks to like, catch drunk drivers and stuff. Kinda weird time to do that now, though."

"Good thing I don't get drunk before four then, right, kids?" the woman asked. When they all stared, she added, "Joke."

Kaylee surely hoped so. The woman pulled out into the street and began her merge into the steady slow lane of traffic on the street where they'd seen Carl a few minutes before. Kaylee's head twisted in every direction, trying to catch a glimpse of her persecutor. There were no sudden dramatic changes in vision, no strange chords of music, no colors or prickly sensations. Just people in the street who were glistening with sweat, and traffic. Ramon had been looking around as well, but after he, too, found no signs of immediate danger, he studied Kaylee's face. "You sick or something?"

"Sick of this stupid mess," she said in a low voice. "But no. Why?"

"Your nose." She rubbed at it, horrified that something gross might be hanging from a nostril. "No, it's all twitchin'. Like a bunny. It's kinda cute."

She sniffed again, hiding her pleasure. The peppery weed smell still lingered. She'd thought it had been something to do with the woman's voice, but their chauffeur was too busy peering around the line of traffic to talk. Maybe it had been something from the alley, or an odor they'd picked up from the Dumpsters. "Just a weird smell," she told him. "It's okay."

"You sure? Because . . . " For a few seconds she hoped he might take her hand again, but he halted in mid-reach. "Cool, then. You know how to take care of yourself." Had he wanted to say something else? Ramon turned his head abruptly away, scanning the streets.

Rosa, in the meanwhile, had finally extricated a CD from the player. "M.C. Fugly," she read from the disc. She looked back up at the woman driver. "My violin teacher says rap music is the mouthpiece of the culturally bereft."

The woman snatched the CD and tossed it over her shoulder. "Yeah, that's why I'm giving it up. You should, too. Bad for you." *Zip.* A tiny silver Frisbee nearly sliced off Kaylee's ear before it clattered to a rest behind the back headrests.

What in the world was this woman *on?* Kaylee scarcely had time to think the ungrateful thought before Rosa sang out, "Big head, two o'clock!"

"What?" said the woman, startled.

"It's way after three, baby." Ramon tried to catch a glimpse of Kaylee's watch.

Kaylee knew exactly what Rosa was telling them. Ahead of the car and to the right, Carl was emerging from a florist's. She caught herself staring at his enormous pink brow and his darting eyes before she realized that he was less than a dozen feet away. "Crap!" she snarled, throwing as much of herself as possible into the gap between the front and back seats. As an afterthought, she reached up, grabbed Ramon by the collar of his T-shirt, and hauled him down after her.

He landed atop her with a whuff of surprise. Their faces were an inch apart. She could smell his skin and its faint traces of soap and cheap aftershave mingled with the faintest spice of drying sweat. Downy hairs grew on his upper lip. He still stared at her in shock. "Carl." She mouthed the word rather than spoke it. As close as they were, it was all she needed to do. Beneath her back, the car rumbled as they pulled forward another few feet.

Ramon's eyes widened. They really were the most impossible brown, the shade of autumn leaves or strong tea, as soft and comforting as a friendly dog's. Not that Ramon was a dog. He didn't have floppy ears or chew bones, or have a tongue. No, that was silly. Of course he had a tongue. Why was she thinking about his tongue? It's not like she was obsessed with it. Was she?

Could he read her mind? The boy's lips spread into a smile, sweet and gentle. No. It was only because they were so close, and because she had been staring at him. "I'm sorry," she whispered.

He laughed slightly, and shook his head. "I'm not."

"What are you two doing back there?" she heard the woman ask, a note of worry in her voice.

"Kissing up on each other," Rosa informed her. At the woman's startled response, she added, "Mommy says it's a bad influence on me, but they're at it all the time anyway because they don't really care if I grow up to be emotionally stunted."

Ramon rolled his eyes dramatically, suppressing his laughter with a series of snorts. Then without warning, he pressed his lips to hers in a quick, experimental kiss, pulling back quickly to judge Kaylee's reaction.

What was her reaction, exactly? For a stunned moment she didn't know. Then, overwhelmed by the scent of honeysuckle, she reached up with her mouth and kissed him back. Their lips parted, gently searching for the other's. It was wrong—so wrong. But Kaylee didn't want it to stop.

"Gross!" she heard from above. When Kaylee opened her eyes once more and tilted her head, she could see Rosa staring down at them, lip curled with disgust. "Big head's gone now. And I *knew* you was kissing up on each other!"

Ramon sat up first, craning his neck to seek any traces of Carl. By the time he extended his hand to help Kaylee back to her seat, the woman had launched into a lecture. "You two can't be doing that while we go through the police block! I need you both to sit up and behave. Please." Her tone had changed. Gone was the vagueness of before; she was direct and even a little bossy. "Let me do all the talking," she warned them, rolling down her window. "Don't contradict a word I say."

"Sorry," Kaylee automatically apologized. She wiped off her lips and sat as far away from Ramon as she could in the back seat. She hadn't really kissed him, had she? While Carl was nearby? What in the world was *wrong* with her? Kaylee caught the driver peering at her in the rear-view mirror. The woman must think she was some kind of weird, psycho, freak girl!

If that was the case, though, the woman didn't say a word about it when she stuck out her head through the window. "Hi, Officer!" she said in a bright, chirpy tone. "How about this blackout, huh?" Kaylee could only see a blue-clad torso from where she sat, but behind the policeman were a number of other officers talking to each other or to their headquarters over the police radio. The man bent down, revealing a bristly moustache and a pair of sunglasses as dark as the woman's. He turned his head to scan the car's interior. "I was taking the kids home from their music lessons," she told him. When he didn't answer, she asked, "Is everything okay?"

"We're checking reports of some suspicious activities in this area," the policeman said levelly.

"Definitely nothing suspicious about us." The woman laughed. "Just me and the kids." Kaylee sniffed, close to sneezing from the weird and pungent smell that had been plaguing her since she set foot in the car. "And my little girl's got to pee."

All four of them waited through a long, expectant pause before Rosa finally picked up her cue. "Real bad," she informed the officer. She sounded grumpy.

"License and registration?"

The question, baldly asked, seemed to stun the woman for a moment. "Oh, sure," she finally said. "Now where did I . . . " Once again she lowered both visors and looked through the flaps, and then grappled with the latch to the glove compartment. "You know, I could swear I had them yesterday," she said, not sounding certain about it.

"Maybe in your purse?" Kaylee's suggestion drew no response. Did the woman even have a purse? Kaylee hadn't seen one.

"Dios!" Ramon had been looking out of the car's rear window. "There's your friend again," he whispered. Kaylee whipped her head around, frightened. Carl was emerging from some sort of tiny convenience

store immediately next to the florist's, back down the street. He looked around, obviously in search of something. Specifically, in search of them. They had to get *moving*.

"Mommy!" Rosa reeled out the word with maximum emphasis on the whininess. Kaylee's already tattered nerves frayed a few inches more from the whiplike annoyance of it. "I gotta *go*."

The woman was too busy searching in the glove compartment to realize that Rosa was talking to her. "Oh!" she said at last, startled. "Don't worry, um . . . Wanda. We'll find you a restroom soon."

For a moment it had looked like Carl might walk in the opposite direction. Instead, he took a look at the cluster of police cars and began to walk toward them. Why? What could he do? It wasn't as if he could drag Kaylee out of the car and demand the police hand her over, could he? No, she thought. But he could get her in a lot of trouble. He could tell the police she was concealing her dad's ATM card in her pocket, for starters, and there'd be questions, and her dad would find out, and . . . She didn't like where that train of thought led. Rosa's whining, tiresome voice made her more antsy. Kaylee would have given almost anything for the anxiety of a couple of minutes before, when the worst thing she had to worry about was whether or not Ramon was about to kiss her.

"I gotta go *now!*" The little girl began squirming around in her seat and kicking her legs like she was riding a bicycle. *"I'm gonna pee in my pants! I'm gonna pee in my pants! I'm gonna explooooooode!"*

"Holy crap," said the policeman, withdrawing his

face from the window, as if Rosa might make good on her promise and spray him in the face. "Ma'am, pass on through. And have your license and registration readily available in the future, please."

"Oh, thank you, Officer," said the woman, raising her voice over Rosa's dramatics. "Hold on, pumpkin. Thank you again!" she added in the false, chirpy voice while she rolled up the window.

Ahead of the police block, the road was relatively clear. "Hah!" said the woman, her voice back to normal. She looked in the mirror and stepped on the accelerator. Parked cars and buildings began to whiz by in a blur. They were actually making headway!

"Good work, *princesa*," said Ramon over the seat.

"I know," she replied. "But why is it whenever we're in a hurry I got to pretend I got to pee? Is that the best you people can do? I'm ten. I *am* potty-trained, you know."

Kaylee couldn't see Carl any longer. She hefted herself down into the seat once more and sighed. The waves of cool washing over her were either the Grand Marquis's blasting air conditioner or deep relief. She couldn't tell, and she didn't care which.

"And why do I have to be named *Wanda?* I don't look like a *Wanda*. Do I look like a *Wanda?*" Rosa asked, obviously annoyed.

"That's what was on the tip of her tongue, baby," Ramon told her, rubbing her shoulder from behind. "She didn't mean you looked like a Wanda. So where is it you want to go, lady?" he asked the driver.

Once more the woman tilted her head so she could look into the mirror behind her. "Oh, I know where I'm going, now," she assured him. Near the upcoming intersection, where traffic began to clog, she swerved onto another less crowded street, clipping the right rear tire against the curb with a jolt.

"Well, why did *Wanda* have to be on the tip of her tongue?" Rosa wanted to know.

"You ask an awful lot of questions," the woman replied.

" 'Cause I want to know stuff," Rosa said. "Like, what's your name?"

"You don't need to know that," snapped the woman.

"My violin teacher says the same thing. Okay, how about like, how can you drive this car if you don't got any keys in it?"

Ramon leaned forward. "What? Don't be craz—uh-oh."

Kaylee had a terrible sense that right as things were suddenly going so well, they were about to go horribly wrong again. She leaned forward and peered around the driver's seat to see what had actually silenced Ramon's tongue. Sure enough, where there should have been a set of keys dangling from the ignition, there was nothing. Beneath the steering column, though, where the plastic had been broken away, hung a bundle of multicolored wires, some stripped and twisted together, that had been dislodged when the car had hit the curb.

"That," said the woman as she floored the accelerator, "was the wrong question."

3:42 P.M.

"Lady, why don't you stop the car and let us out?" Kaylee wasn't sure which frightened her more: their dangerous speed or the look of sheer fear that paled Ramon's dark skin. He spoke in the same calming voice he'd used on everyone from Mr. Cloutier to the panicking businesspeople outside the skyscraper, yet he clutched the back of the woman's seat as if frightened that at any minute all four of them might suddenly be catapulted through the front windshield. His attention was fixed on Rosa. For once, the little girl was quiet, her eyes big. She clutched her violin and little backpack from behind the safety of her seat belt, as if they could protect her. "Come on, I've got my little sister to think about. You don't want anything to happen to her."

"Ramon?" said Rosa, the single word a more heart-rending plea for help than anything Kaylee had ever heard.

Where in the world were they going? It didn't matter

to the woman what kind of road lay ahead. Alleyway, narrow street, or broad avenue, if they looked reasonably empty, the woman took them. She seemed to have a destination in mind. Although she occasionally doubled back to avoid traffic, they headed in a single general direction. Kaylee couldn't tell which direction, though. No familiar city landmarks loomed over the tops of the decaying buildings that leaned in from every side. Kaylee couldn't sit by and let herself be kidnapped to God knew where by some maniac, though. They had to do something! "You used us to get through that police block," she bargained, shouting above the roar of the engine. Her nose still tickled; she sniffed it clear. "I think we can call us even. Let us out!"

"We don't care if you've been jackin' cars," Ramon agreed. Kaylee was relieved that she'd hit on a strategy he approved. "We helped you. Now you help us. Just let us out." The woman merely shot him a look over her sunglasses in the mirror.

"We won't tell anybody," promised Kaylee. She wouldn't, either. Who could she tell? Her dad? The woman could spend the rest of her life stealing cars for all Kaylee cared. "Pull over and let us out!"

After a long silence in which it seemed as if the woman was thinking over the offer, she at last opened her mouth. It closed again so she could jerk the wheel and swerve around a battery of orange trucks clustered around a gushing fire hydrant. A spray of water leapt into the air when they splashed through the flooded street, sending water showering down onto the car with a percussive pounding that jarred Kaylee's molars. Flicking on the wipers, the woman spoke. "I thought you good Christians wanted a ride."

"Come on," urged Ramon, trying to sound pleasant. "We're kids. Who we gonna tell? Even if we wanted to, we gotta keep our profile low," he added, sounding inspired. "Yeah. Because we jack cars, too."

Kaylee's head jerked around. Was he *crazy?* The woman must have thought the same thing; she sounded as if she was laughing at a joke when she said, "Oh, you do, huh?"

"Hell yeah," he said, trying to sound tough. Kaylee recognized this voice too. It was the cocky, macho Ramon she'd first met in the elevator. How many different Ramons were in that head of his? "Everybody who's anybody's heard of us. We got a reputation."

"Oh, yeah? A reputation?" The woman still sounded as if she might snicker at any minute.

Rosa found her voice again. "My big brother is *dangerous.* He makes our mama cry."

"So, do you belong to a gang or something, kid?"

"Yeah."

The woman noticed the long pause. "Does it have a name?"

"Of *course* it has a name!" Rosa spat back. "It's, uh . . . "

"We keep it on the down low," said Kaylee. Her attempt at toughness came out sounding more like a head cold.

Yet Ramon shot her an approving glance. "Yeah, you know it don't pay to advertise in this business."

Rosa, however, spoke up from the front seat. "It's

the Lemley gang. Yeah, I said it," she shot back in challenge when Ramon made a face. Then, to the woman, who was simultaneously dodging traffic and trying to look around at all three of them, "What, you never heard of Marie Lemley? Don't be blaming me 'cause you're out of the loop. And don't give me that look, lady. I ain't the brains. I'm just the cute little decoy girl. How do you know we ain't jacking *you?*"

"Rosa," said Ramon. It sounded like a warning.

Kaylee couldn't help but agree with him. The top of Rosa's backpack sat wide open, and the top of the oversized concerto stuck out. Another inch more and the woman would be able to read the name of their so-called gang leader right on the music's cover. What could they do, though? They were simply *sitting* there and letting this criminal drive them to some kind of— she didn't want to think about how bad it could get. All because they'd broken that most cardinal of rules passed from parent to child: Never get in a stranger's car. "Come on, lady," Kaylee said, still trying to mask the fear she didn't want quivering in her words. "Let us out. You don't want to hurt us and get Marie the Mauler mad at you."

The woman said nothing. She roared around the corner and skidded the car to a stop in front of a low gray building, long deserted and neglected, huddled among a number of similar old buildings crowded close together. All the structures looked empty, as if they'd been condemned. "Don't move a damned muscle," she warned them, when all three of them reached for their door handles.

Ramon's eyes popped wide when the woman suddenly tugged at the collar of her knit blouse, reached inside, and started digging in her bra. What did she have in there, besides the obvious? The bitter, peppery smell made Kaylee's eyes water, but when the woman withdrew a dark object from inside her clothing, she thought she recognized it immediately—a small gun. The woman pointed it at Rosa.

Kaylee felt as if an icy hand had wrapped itself around her lungs and squeezed the breath from her body. Every instinct told her that Rosa's life was in danger. "Duck!" Kaylee yelled.

Time seemed to slow to a crawl. Every heartbeat sounded deeper, more ominous, like the double bang of a timpani followed by measures and measures of rests before the next. Kaylee's hand reached out through the gap in the front seats and connected with the top of Rosa's head, shoving the little girl down and forward and out of harm's way. The woman's wrist snaked out and dipped; she squeezed the ominous object clutched in her fingers.

When time snapped back to normal, Kaylee's skin crawled with a thousand small insects. She felt as if someone had slapped her with a wet towel. Had she saved Rosa? She could scarcely bear to look, in case she had acted too late.

"Ow!" said the girl, rubbing her forehead from where it had banged lightly against the dashboard. "Are you *crazy?*"

In her hand, the woman still held the object she'd pulled from inside her shirt. She still pointed it in the direction of the passenger seat, but not at Rosa—at the building where the car had coasted to a stop.

"What's the matter with this thing?" snarled the woman, jabbing at the biggest of its three buttons.

It was a garage door opener. The woman hadn't been going to shoot Rosa at all; she'd only been aiming the plastic device at the oversized bay door at the building's side. Crap. Could she be any stupider?

"It's okay." She felt a hand on her wrist. Ramon's eyes were wide; his nostrils flared as breath after breath forced its way through them. He seemed to be sucking in air as if he, too, had suffered a moment's shock. Did her own face look even a fraction as frightened as his did? In a whisper, he rasped out, "Thank you."

All she could do was nod. With a choice swear word, their captor tossed the remote so that it bounced off the dashboard, clattered against the front window, and landed on the floor. "What's the matter with the stupid thing?" she yelled.

Rosa, still holding her forehead, seemed unimpressed by the woman's fit of temper. "It's not gonna work without electricity. You the one that's *stupid.*"

The woman raised a hand abruptly, as if about to slap Rosa for the backtalk. This time both Ramon and Kaylee flinched forward, ready to defend the girl. Instead, the woman merely slammed her fist down onto the car horn, letting out a blast of angry noise. Again and again she jabbed at the horn until after what seemed like forever, the door started to rise. Someone on the other side raised it in fits and starts, the door's weight preventing it from being lifted in one go. "That's better," the woman growled. She floored the accelerator. Up and over the short driveway they all went in a daredevil leap, the Grand Marquis bouncing onto the concrete on the other side before plunging into darkness.

The sound of the door's descent, metallic and grating, set Kaylee's teeth on edge. It was a dentist's drill into her teeth's juicy roots, heightened by the terror she felt when the door's heavy edge guillotined the last sliver of daylight. "Ramon?" she heard Rosa say from the front seat.

"I'm here for you, baby," he replied, his voice light but strained. Kaylee's heart began to ache with fear and yearning. Where was someone for her? As if sensing her need, she felt Ramon's fingers grope for her own. They squeezed, warm and comforting. She'd only known Ramon for four hours, but in a situation like this, a squeeze was exactly what she needed. "Just you sit tight."

Kaylee heard the sound of a latch; the car's dome lamps flickered on without warning. Ramon's face was inches away—she could see his eyes trying to focus in the unexpected light. The woman unfastened her belt and simultaneously whipped around to look over the seat; for a moment it sounded as if her twisting neck had let off the metallic clack. "You," she said to Ramon. "Yeah, you," she added, when he reared back in surprise. "Gang leader. Come with me."

"I ain't comin' with you," Ramon protested. "I don't know what's gonna happen if I get out!"

What had happened to the vague, disorganized woman they'd first met? "You'll find out what'll happen if you don't. And you won't like it. You want to risk it?" Obviously that woman had been left behind at the barricade. "You two sit here," she told the girls. "If you move, I can't guarantee your friend's safety."

"Ramon?" said Rosa, worried.

"The girls won't go anywhere," Ramon growled. Kaylee could tell he hated being in this position. "It's not like they can see where they're goin', anyway. Who'd *volunteer* to wander around *in the dark?*" He raised his eyebrows.

Why the strange emphasis? Was there something he'd wanted her to understand? Of course Kaylee re-membered what Ramon had said earlier about victims and volunteers. The distinction had been nagging her all day; even a few moments before she'd wished they could *do* something rather than let the woman drive them all into danger. What in the world should she be doing now? Why would she volunteer to walk around in the darkness?

The answer came to her so unexpectedly that she wanted to strike herself on the forehead. It was so simple—the dome lights were casting a pool of illumi-nation all around the car. All she had to do was turn her head to see any number of details about their im-mediate surroundings!

She couldn't be obvious about it. Though Kaylee pretended to stare at the woman, between blinks she let her eyes dart rapidly about to memorize as much as possible about what she saw. The driver's side of the car opened next to a wall hung with all kinds of tools, both power and hand-operated. Another wall stood a few yards in front of the Grand Marquis; against it were stacked numbers of tires and boxes of wheel covers. Kaylee didn't dare look on the passenger side, because for the first time since they had seen her, the woman removed her sunglasses and looked directly at Kaylee. Her eyes were far older than Kaylee would have guessed; they made the woman look mean. "They'd better not go anywhere if they know what's good for them," she snapped before turning away. "Now move it."

"Ramon . . . " Fear reduced Rosa to a whimper.

"It'll be okay, *princesa*," he told her. Kaylee listened to his reassurances without looking at either of them. She was too busy gauging the distance between the car and a flight of concrete steps a short distance away from the car's hood. "I'll be right back. Do everything Kaylee says, okay?" Rosa nodded. "I won't be gone long at all."

"I'm waiting," said the woman, her heels sliding across the concrete. Kaylee whipped her head around and caught a quick glimpse of the garage's layout to her right—and was immediately glad she had, for on the car's other side lay a square-mouthed hole in the floor like a service pit in a quick oil change place. Kaylee shivered. If she'd fallen into that in the dark, she wouldn't have to worry ever again about what her dad had in store for her. A floor littered with car parts led to a confusing jumble of doors and windows in the far distance. Probably offices. A man with a flashlight waited in the shadows. Had he been the one to open and lower the loading bay door? Probably.

Kaylee strained to see something more of the man,

but without warning, the front door banged shut. The dome lights in the car blinked out. Had she seen enough? She certainly hoped so.

She felt a pair of lips against her ear. They were Ramon's, warm and sweet, followed by his fingers gently pressed on her mouth, to keep her from talking. "Take care of Rosa." His words were measured, barely whispered, mere stirrings of air. "Whatever happens to me." She couldn't speak with Ramon's hand in the way; Kaylee merely nodded, afraid to make a noise. Was he really leaving them all alone? What did he expect her to do? "Do what you got to. Promise me," she heard him say.

Promise him what? How could she take care of a little girl who didn't like her? What in the world could she do? Ramon trusting her with Rosa was like the Queen of England tossing Kaylee the crown jewels in a paper grocery bag, but it was painfully obvious Ramon loved his treasure much more than the Queen. Did he really trust Kaylee that much? What if she disappointed him?

She didn't want to. She couldn't disappoint him.

"It'll be okay," she told Ramon. Letting go of his hand—the only solid connection she had to the boy in that dark space—was one of the hardest things she had ever done.

"Yeah," he said. "It'll be okay. I'll be right back, *princesa*. Just hold tight."

"Promise?"

Before he could answer, Kaylee heard the woman's shoes crunch across the gritty garage floor. "So sweet," she said, both words sounding bitter on the tongue. "That's enough."

"I'll be right back," Ramon promised. His last words bounced from the nearby wall, hollow and faint. Far to the right side, Kaylee watched as the man's flashlight beam bounced over the cluttered floor, reflecting off bits of chrome and metal ripped from stolen cars while the man holding it lit a path for the two new arrivals.

Kaylee peered out the window, her heart racing every time she saw the woman's black shoes picking their way across the floor. "I'm scared," she heard from the front seat.

"It's okay, honey." There was no way in the world Kaylee sounded as if she meant it. She cleared her voice and tried to be more reassuring. "See? Look, there are your brother's sneakers over there. They're going to the office to talk." Without warning, the flashlight shone in her direction. From the garage's far end it could not have cast much light. She wondered if Ramon could see her face through the window, pale and worried. The beam flicked back, and for a moment Kaylee could see Ramon's brown legs climbing steps along the other wall. "Rosa?" she asked, when the last glimmer of light had disappeared. "Rosa?" she asked again, when she didn't get an answer.

"What?" She could tell from the quiver in the girl's voice that she was no longer the smart-mouthed back-talker, or the mealymouthed charmer. What Kaylee heard was the tremble of a scared little girl.

"Hand me your violin case." Didn't the girl hear her? "Pick up and give me—*ow!*" Bright white fireworks exploding at the front of her skull—Rosa's violin case had accidentally bashed against her forehead. "Okay, I deserved that," she said, groping blindly for the case's handle.

"Sorry."

"No worries." It hadn't been that hard a blow. More a surprise than anything, truthfully. Kaylee set the violin on the floor beside her feet. "Now your backpack."

"You're not going to leave me, too, are you?" Rosa's question was the most mournful thing Kaylee had ever heard.

"No, I'm not. I promise." Kaylee fell silent for a moment while she grappled with the backpack's confusing straps. "Now, let's get you into the back seat so you don't have to be up there in the dark by yourself," she suggested. "Can you take my hand?"

Kaylee heard the click of a seat belt unfastening. "I'm not scared of the *dark*. Or anything else," the little girl said with scorn. "But if it makes *you* feel better . . . " That comment alone made Kaylee a touch happier; dealing with stubborn Rosa at least gave her a slight sense of normalcy. The girl's hair smelled like shampoo and soap when Kaylee half-pulled, half-assisted her over the console in the car's center. "I'm not going to sit on your *lap*," Rosa complained, once most of her was in the back seat. "What are you, some kind of weirdo? It ain't enough you gotta be kissin' up on my brother, you gotta kiss up on me, too?"

"Get your elbow out of my face!" Kaylee suggested. It was nearly impossible to tell what part of the youngest Pastor was where, but a moment later they had managed to disentangle themselves. "And I wish you'd stop saying I kiss up on your brother."

"You do!" said Rosa in the tone of the indignant. "I saw! He used to be a *good* boy! Never kissed up on girls until he met you!"

"Wait—what?" Kaylee paused, startled, wanting to know more. "He doesn't kiss up on lots of girls? Or get their phone numbers?"

"He's not all oversexed like *some* white girls," Rosa said in a mutter.

Hmmm. Interesting, if true, but Kaylee had to set that information aside for later. "Well, the kissing's not going to be happening again." Kaylee felt better with someone close by, and Rosa's tidbit almost made her feel affectionate toward the girl. "Let's figure out what we're going to do now."

"Do? We're supposed to sit still. The lady said so."

"And your brother told me to protect you. We're going to get out of here." That was what Ramon had wanted her to do, right? Why would he have suggested she get a good look at their surroundings if he didn't intend for her to do something about their situation?

"But Ramon!"

"We won't leave him," she promised. "We'd never leave him behind." She didn't know how, but they'd all get out of that garage with their skins intact. This might have been the worst situation she'd ever been in—being expelled looked like a freakin' picnic, now—but the garage was an obstacle course, exactly like the ones she'd run with her father for years, just darker and scarier. You didn't think about how you were going to tackle a mud pit farther on when you were trying to vault a wall immediately in front of you. "Get your backpack. I'll carry your violin." For good measure, she added, "And don't talk until I say it's okay!"

Ramon had left the back door of the Grand Marquis ajar. Good. Kaylee wouldn't have to worry about anyone overhearing it swing open, or fret about triggering the lights. It took a moment of careful maneuvering in the dark to stand up and get her balance, especially with the violin in tow. Only by keeping her free hand on the car could she keep her orientation. "Give me your hand," she whispered, groping for Rosa. Their fingers met in mid-air; Kaylee grabbed hold, helping the little girl slide from the car.

Shutting the door behind them would be foolishness itself, especially if they had to give up and come back. Kaylee pushed it to, but only enough so that it wouldn't gouge them as they moved past. The path to the concrete stairs was a straight shot from the car's left side. Of course, what she thought was a straight line in the dark might be entirely different from an actual straight line, but at least she had the car and wall to guide her most of the way. A general idea of the wall, at any rate—she didn't dare run a hand along it for fear of disturbing the tools she'd seen hanging there. The possibility of cutting off a finger also kept her left hand tightly wrapped around the violin case's handle as she led them forward.

Rosa kept a tight grip on her other hand, clutching so hard that Kaylee's right fingers began to balloon from the pressure. Kaylee started a slow, tentative rhythm forward, shuffling with her leading foot, then dragging the other and Rosa behind. The first few steps were easy enough, with an elbow tapping against the Grand Marquis's cool metal exterior. Then her foot encountered some sort of dense object—a tire leaning against the wall at an angle, she discovered by lightly bouncing the violin case on its rubbery surface. She shifted slightly closer to the car and eased them both around it.

The car's hood dipped lower and lower as they moved forward, until at last Kaylee felt its rounded nose against her knee. How far ahead were the stairs? She searched in her memory. Ten feet? Twelve? That was nothing, right? How long did it take her to walk a dozen feet out in the open? Mere seconds.

Inch by inch she crept forward. *Shuffle-step. Shuffle-step.* Rosa followed behind, her breathing the only sound she made. Too many questions cluttered her head. How many shuffles made a yard? Five? Ten? Where were the steps? Had she veered, in the darkness? Was she leading them closer and closer to that awful pit in the room's middle? What if the floor they were crossing was as cluttered and sloppy as the rest? What she'd seen had been chaos, but then again, if this was one of those places where criminals brought stolen cars so they could be taken to bits for their parts, or repainted and sold back out onto the streets, she could hardly expect it to be a spread from *Good Housekeeping.*

She kicked something—a nut or a bolt or a washer, by the sound of it. She hadn't felt it against her foot. At its tinkling, high-pitched ringing as it rolled across the cement, Kaylee halted. Surely such a tiny, tiny sound wouldn't attract anyone's attention.

"I didn't do it," she heard from behind her. Kaylee squeezed Rosa's fingers in reassurance. "Well, I didn't!"

"I know! Just keep quiet!" Kaylee whispered back. "We have—"

From the other side of the garage, Kaylee heard the sounds of voices raised. The woman and the man were arguing. Tiny cyclones of rage seemed to swirl around her, invisible yet nonetheless fearsome. In the darkness, without a single pinpoint of light to guide her, she felt vulnerable.

Obstacle course, she reminded herself. This whole incident was one more obstacle. She had to keep her eyes on the horizon, to focus on her ultimate goal. She wasn't helpless. She had all her senses to guide her.

Shuffle-step. Shuffle-step. Kaylee's foot struck the corner of something hard and solid. She let go of Rosa to reach out and grab whatever it was. To her relief, her fingers scraped hard against the rough texture of concrete and metal. They'd reached the stairs; Kaylee's foot had collided with the bottom step's corner. An inch or two to the right and they would have missed them altogether. She didn't want to think about that. She'd succeeded. It was easy enough to bend over and grope across the stair's surface; she was relieved that save for a paint can on the bottom stair against the wall, the first few steps were clear of everything but a layer of grit. Kaylee once again took Rosa's hand and guided it to the concrete, letting the girl know their location. Up they went, doubled over, until after sixteen stairs they reached a landing at the top.

It would get trickier from there. What if there was

no exit? What if . . . hard as it was, Kaylee squelched down all her doubts. She had Rosa to care for. And why would there be stairs if there was no exit? After a few false starts, her hands finally found the wall, running over some cylindrical tubes that fed into some kind of metal box. A fuse or breaker box, she guessed. To the right was some kind of railing—good, because she didn't want to plummet over the edge in case she made a misstep. And to the left . . .

A doorknob. Attached to a genuine, honest-to-God wooden door. Kaylee wanted to yank it open and run through as fast as possible, but she had to be careful. Flooding the room with light if there was a window on the other side would accomplish nothing except drawing attention to them. There was no bright slash of sunshine from underneath the door's crack, so she twisted the knob and hoped for the best.

It turned. The door unlatched and swung open a fraction of an inch. Though the garage had been pitch black, the space on the door's other side seemed to be merely a dark gray. "Follow me," she whispered to Rosa. "But still be quiet, okay?"

She made sure the knob wasn't locked before she pulled it to, once they were on the other side. Light was coming from someplace distant, though precious little of it trickled down their way. Still, it was more than they'd had before, and enough to see the difference between shadow and solid. Although a door immediately opposite the one they'd just passed through proved to be locked tight, a narrower staircase led up another flight in an angle away from the landing. "My violin," Rosa asked. "You didn't lose it?"

"I've got it right here. Let's go."

Moving from darkness to dusk felt like surfacing from underwater. It became obvious, when they reached the next landing, that the light had been coming from a window on the building's other side, where it sat mostly covered with a crooked, dusty blind at the end of a long hallway. It was hotter up here too— stifling, really, as if the upstairs hadn't seen fresh air in years. Kaylee could take the heat and the smell of sawdust and old newspapers. A shut-up, condemned building on a scorching afternoon meant that they weren't likely to run into anyone, and that was what mattered most at the moment. Rosa started immediately to tread down the hall, but Kaylee grabbed her before she could take a step. The hallway floorboards, wooden and worn, were over the side of the building where their kidnapper and her accomplice had gone. She didn't want them hearing noises from parts of the building that were supposed to be abandoned. That would be asking for trouble.

Up the final flight of stairs they went, where it ended at a last door. At first it seemed not to want to budge, but under the weight of Kaylee's body it gave way slightly. She risked a grunt and a heave to heft it open. Her eyes began watering when the sun's unfiltered rays struck her face; the door had swung out onto the building's rooftop. Waves of heat rose from the tarred, pebbly surface. As far as Kaylee could see were other roofs, and the tops of trees, and in the far distance, shimmering like a desert mirage, the faint outlines of skyscrapers. Amazing, how loud the world sounded to her ears.

"It's *hot*," Rosa complained, once she'd stepped onto the surface.

Kaylee's immediate instinct was to shush her, but it was safe to talk up here. They were outdoors; their voices wouldn't carry downstairs if she shut the door. "Are you okay?" When Rosa nodded, Kaylee reached to run her fingers across the girl's brow. "Does your head hurt?"

With a bob of her dark head, Rosa wrenched away. "Get *off!*" They still weren't friends, even after all that. Okay. Fine. They didn't have to be. Kaylee still had a responsibility for her. She began to look around the roof, pretending it was one of her dad's camping missions and she'd been sent ahead to survey an area. "Now go back and get Ramon," Rosa demanded.

"Not yet." Kaylee's voice came out sounding surprisingly authoritative. A lot like her dad's, in fact. She started to pace the roof, avoiding the pipes and other obvious footfalls while trying to figure out a hiding place. Someone had abandoned a bunch of painting supplies. The tarp covering them had long ago rotted at the seams, exposing a number of corroded cans and an old wooden ladder. "I promised I'd get you somewhere safe."

"This is safe!" Rosa said. "And I want my damned violin back."

"Fine." Kaylee abandoned that corner of the rooftop and handed back the case. Her fingers were tired of clutching it, anyhow. "All yours." She stomped over to the building's other side, aware that the rubber soles of her sneakers seemed to be melting into the sun-baked roof. She didn't need synesthesia to tell her it was hot. Between her watering eyes, the acidic smell of the gooey black tar, and the burning of her skin from the sun's unrelenting rays, her normal senses were already working overtime. But her condition was active anyway, sending pulsating oranges and yellows to her skin. Maybe there was some sort of fire escape? She could see one on the back of the next building over.

Rosa didn't seem at all happy at Kaylee's quick concession. "I *said*, go get my brother!"

"Listen." Kaylee whipped around and pointed a finger at Rosa. "I've tried being nice to you. I got your butt out of that car, you're welcome very much." Even as she lost her temper, she knew it was wrong. The day's temperature wasn't the girl's fault . . . although the fact that they'd been abducted was. Partly, anyway. "But what happens if I leave you up here by yourself without someplace to hide, and one of those car thieves comes up looking for us? Do you want to risk that? Never mind. Frankly, I don't really care whether you do or not, because I'm not going to leave you exposed up here. It's like a desert. You know what happens to people in deserts, out in the sun? They get dehydrated and collapse and die in no time. Then your brother would kill me." Did the savage stab of dislike Rosa shot her way mean the girl wanted to see Ramon engage in a little friendly murder? "So deal with it."

This building didn't seem to have been built with a fire escape—or else it had fallen off long ago. Why couldn't they have been stranded in the next building over? Not only did it have a sturdy-looking series of ladders and platforms scaling down its back, but someone had built a series of greenhouses across its length. Most of the panes of glass were missing, but the structures provided at least some shade on the far side. Kaylee could see an old plastic lawn chair abandoned near the stairwell door, as a bonus. Compared to this rooftop, that building was crowned by a green and grassy oasis. It was all the more frustrating that the buildings were so close together. If they hadn't been four stories up, she could almost have jumped the seven or eight feet across.

"Whatever. Get your rear in gear." Rosa used her backpack to cast shade on her face.

"I know!" Thinking about obstacle courses had given Kaylee an inspired idea. She raced back over to the pile of rotting painting supplies. The last shreds of tarp were easy to rip. Years of sun and weather had reduced its creases to whitened tatters. "Put down your stuff and help me a minute." Rosa heaved the sigh of a long-suffering saint, obeyed, then daintily marched over. "Help me with this," Kaylee told her.

The ladder looked sturdy enough; whatever wood had gone into its construction had neither cracked nor splintered from the elements. Kaylee could probably have handled it on her own, but Rosa's assistance would make things easier. "What crazy idea is in your head?" Rosa's voice rose about a half octave.

"Come on!" Kaylee sprinted to the roof's opposite end, dragging the ladder—and a balking Rosa, it felt like—behind her. "It's more than long enough. We can get you over there, safe and sound, where it's shady, and . . . "

"*Chúpeme!*" Rosa spat, stopping in her tracks. It

didn't matter. Kaylee was already standing the ladder up on its end by the roof's ledge. She could tell it would reach, with ample overhang on either side. "Oh, no!"

"Rosa, you've got to trust me on this." The ladder was heavy, but nothing she couldn't handle. Hadn't she hauled around eighty-pound knapsacks for longer periods of time? The only thing she worried about was having the ladder bounce and rebound out of control, if she dropped it onto the other ledge from too high a height. She grabbed onto one of the upper rungs and slowly eased it forward, keeping the feet from slipping by bracing her leg against one of them. "I do this kind of thing all the time with my dad." Never at quite this height, but the principle was the same, right? "Nothing bad will happen. It's easy."

"I don't *care* what kind of crazy stuff you white people do with your daddies," Rosa said in a frenzy. Kaylee attempted to shush her with her back turned. Though it was safer to talk up here, she didn't know for sure how far their voices might carry. "I ain't crossing that thing."

Kaylee had to wait a moment to answer. It was difficult to hold all the weight of the ladder from her end; the most she could hope to do was control its fall. Gravity took over when she had halfway lowered it over the other ledge. The ladder fell with a wooden clatter and recoiled once before landing again. They couldn't have heard the noise down below, could they? Kaylee's hands stung from the impact, but she ignored the pain. They had an impromptu bridge between the two buildings. "Yes, you are," she said. "It's for your own good."

"There's no way it's gonna be good," said Rosa, once more sounding anxious. The ladder seemed sturdy enough. When Kaylee had leaned out and bounced it slightly, she knew it would bear her weight. And if it held her, it certainly would support a single skinny Rosa, if not three.

"You first!" she said, trying to sound cheerful. This scheme really could work. At least, it could if she got Rosa across. "Okay, me first," she suggested, upon seeing Rosa's hostile expression.

"I'll be okay in the sun," Rosa said, following Kaylee across the roof to where she'd left her violin and pack. "I've got extra melanin because I'm *chicana*. I won't burn. It's stuff in the skin that gives you color."

"I know what melanin is," Kaylee responded. She'd recognized the word, at least, though whether she could have dredged it from her memory readily was questionable. If Rosa was as smart as she was good at the violin, she was one talented little girl. What else did she have up her sleeve? Was she training for the Olympic gymnastics team? No wonder Ramon was so protective of her. "Here. Hold the ladder. I'll show you how easy it is."

Standing on the edge was the easy part, so long as she remembered not to look down. Kaylee wasn't particularly frightened of heights, but she'd only really experienced them inside elevators or tall buildings or on the sides of mountains with safety harnesses all around. This was a little bit more frightening—but not too different from the endless Saturdays she'd grown up enduring. "Okay, give me your violin." She expected resistance, but Rosa obediently handed up the case, her hands shaking. "Now the backpack." She slung the latter over her shoulder. Now it *really* felt like a Saturday with her father. "Keep a firm hold on the ladder while I'm on it, okay? Watch what I do."

Kaylee had crossed every type of ladder and bridge known to mankind. She'd been crossing rickety cable ladders before she'd started school. She'd swung across gorges on knotted ropes, navigated long two-by-fours suspended over waist-deep pits of mud. She could cross a single-rope bridge with wire guides faster than most recruits in boot camp. If there was any time she could shine as the army princess she was, it was now. She could do this.

She took a deep breath, fixed her eyes on her goal, and stepped out.

Kaylee never actually remembered the trip between buildings afterward. She simply recalled the relief she felt when she stepped onto the ledge's other side— the fluttery, exultant feeling in the pit of her stomach when she hopped down and realized she'd done it. Yet the actual passage, which should have been frightening and scary, was as anonymous and undistinguished as any of the other bridge crossings she'd made in her life. Was that how soldiers felt, drilled and drilled for months on the mundane, so that their reactions would be automatic when they were finally put to the test? "Balance on the balls of your feet," she suggested. "Don't try to run, but walk normally."

"I can't do that!" Rosa called from the other ledge.

"You can. I did." Rosa shook her head. Kaylee decided to try another tactic. "Yeah, maybe you're right. You're probably too much of a baby."

"I am *not* a baby." The reverse psychology seemed to be working. "I just don't want to."

"Okay. Baby." That was enough to make Rosa leap onto the ledge—a little too quickly, Kaylee realized with dismay. She didn't want the girl trying anything dangerous—or more dangerous than necessary, anyway. "If you don't want to walk across, you can crawl! That might be easier!"

"I *know*." Rosa dropped to her hands and feet, straddling the ladder so that her hands seized the ladder's sides while her feet perched on the rungs. It was awkward but stable. Kaylee held on to the ladder and waited for her to start the crossing. And waited. And waited.

"What's the matter?" she asked at last.

"It's real high," Rosa said in a pitiful voice.

"You're not going to fall," Kaylee said. "Don't look down at the ground." Rosa didn't seem to be able to look anywhere but; she peered over the ledge's precipice with the doomed face of a firing squad victim. Kaylee used her father's voice again. "Rosa! Look at me!" The little girl half-gazed across the gap. Well, it was better than nothing. "I'll talk you across. See if you can take a single step."

Rosa's feet moved forward onto a rung two inches over the ledge, but her hands refused to move. "Sweetie, don't panic. Tell me something. Talk to me."

When Rosa looked up, Kaylee said in desperation, "Tell me about . . . tell me about your mother. What's she doing right now?"

"Working." Rosa seemed relieved to use her mouth again. "She works all the time. She's got like, two jobs."

"See if you can move your hands." Kaylee breathed a sigh of relief when Rosa's hands, one at time, inched forward. "Look up. Look at me. What jobs?"

"She works as a secretary." Rosa reached forward with a foot, braced it against the rung, and inched forward again with her hands. "And then she teaches classes at night for people who don't talk English too good. It's *high*—!"

"Don't look down. Look at me," Kaylee commanded, trying to remain calm. She didn't like watching Rosa's tortuous progress any more than Rosa'd probably enjoyed watching Kaylee prance across. "Where's your daddy?"

"Mount St. Mary's. It's a cemetery," Rosa said. With a small grunt, she moved a little closer.

"Sorry. I guess you must miss him. Keep focused on me, sweetie. I'm right here."

"I *know.*"

She was getting upset again. Best to keep her distracted. "Is it only you and Ramon and your mom, then?"

"There's Manuel."

Oh, yes. The mysterious Manuel. "Another brother, right?"

Rosa took another step. She was completely out in the open now, but she kept her face forward, looking at Kaylee. "He's my older brother. Half brother. We all got the same daddy, but just Ramon and me have our mom."

"And he takes care of you, too?" A few inches more and the girl would be halfway across.

"No. Ramon, he won't let him." Rosa moved forward one more rung. "Well, he hasn't tried *that* hard. Ramon says he's stuck up because he's making lots of money."

"Manuel?"

"Yeah, because he wouldn't give us the time of day until he saw about me in *El Diario*. It's a newspaper."

"You were in the newspaper?" Kaylee was genuinely surprised. "Seriously?"

"Not a *big* article." Even perched fifty feet above the ground on the middle of a wooden ladder, Rosa sounded a little proud of herself. "It was only four and a half inches long. With a photo."

"About your playing?"

"Yeah. I'd quote it to you, but Ramon says talking about myself is conceited." Rosa took another step. "But I *could* quote it to you. If I felt like it."

She was nearly two-thirds of the way across. Nearly there. "Maybe Manuel didn't know how special you were."

"That's the thing. Ramon says that it shouldn't matter whether you got mad talent comin' out the ears or whether you're a stupid mess, family should still stick close to each other." She inched forward more confidently. "So that's why he went to Midtown during my lesson. Because Manuel wanted to, like, help out with this school thing."

"What was Ramon going to tell him?" Kaylee was more interested in the story at this point than she wanted to admit.

"You *must* not know my brother real well if you gotta ask *that*. Of course he's gonna say no! He—" Rosa's left foot slipped. For a brief second Kaylee had a vision of the girl plunging down into the dark, weed-ridden space between the buildings. Her mouth filled with the taste of sour apples. She wanted to reach out and grab Rosa—she was almost that close—but instead she maintained a firm grip on the ladder so that it didn't tip to either side. "Kaylee?" she said, in a very small voice.

Rosa was plainly frightened to death. Her knuckles whitened from clutching onto the ladder. Kaylee could see, though, that the girl's right foot was still firmly planted on its rung. She wasn't going anywhere . . . so long as she didn't panic. "Don't look down," Kaylee told her. "You'll freak out. Look at me, sweetie."

The younger Pastor was contrary enough that she immediately started to look groundward. "It's so high," she wailed. "I'm gonna fall!"

"You are not going to fall. Stop moving your foot around. Put it back down. Next to your other one. Rosa," she added in a firm voice when the girl only flailed it around more. "Put it next to your other one. You're fine. You're almost all the way across."

"Okay," said the girl. "But I'm scared."

"No reason to be scared! You're a few feet away. Come on."

Very tentatively, the girl placed her left foot on the next rung. Could she do it? "I can't," she said. "I can't move." Kaylee knew Rosa could, but fear sometimes made a person do stupid things.

Such as get involved with people like Carl and Annabelle. That was why she'd let them take over her life in the spring, wasn't it? She'd been so afraid of being stuck out in the middle of nowhere, scared and unable to move, that she hadn't taken care to know her supposed new friends before she let them take advantage of her. She should have listened to Brynne Hohensee. Look how long it was taking her to get her footing back from that misstep. "You *can*," Kaylee said. "Look at me. *Look* at me!" When Rosa lifted her chin, Kaylee smiled. "You're almost here. We're practically face to face. A little bit more and you'll never have to do this ever, ever again."

"Promise?"

"Absolutely. Besides, hello? I've got your violin over here. Come and get it before I sell it on eBay."

"You *better* not." Rosa moved forward, her hands just as tense despite the new energy in her voice. "Ramon would kick your butt."

"Just a little . . . that's it. A little more! You're doing great!" Rosa could do it, she knew. Kaylee waited until the girl's knees were completely over the ledge before she let go of the ladder and collected Rosa from it; she clutched Kaylee's neck, hugging it fiercely, unwilling to let go. She could feel Rosa's chest rising and falling with heavy, sobbing breaths. Her neck grew moist with the girl's tears. "It's okay, see?" she said after a moment. "Everything's going to be okay. Don't cry."

"I'm *not* crying," Rosa lied. "But I ain't doing that

again. I don't like it. And I'm gonna tell Ramon you made me do it."

"That's fine. You do that. He'll be doing it himself in a few minutes."

"He'll do it better than *you.*" Rosa was much too heavy to carry indefinitely. Kaylee bent over and deposited her on the rooftop. Collecting the violin case, the backpack, and the chair, and lugging them all over to the shade on the old greenhouse's far side gave Kaylee the perfect excuse not to watch the girl wipe the tears from her eyes and clean up her face with a sleeve. By the time she returned, Rosa was back in fighting condition. "Now go get him already."

"I'm going to. But listen to me; You've got to promise me a couple of things." Kaylee had thought ahead while she'd moved the chair around. "First off—you're going to sit right here and not move. Not move an *inch,*" she ordered, when Rosa opened her mouth to protest. She pushed the girl down into the plastic chair and, for emphasis, picked up the violin and pushed it onto Rosa's lap. "Not until Ramon and I get back."

"How long is that going to take?"

"I wish I had an answer for that, sweetie. Sit tight, no matter what happens. If you have to pee, crouch down up here on the—"

"I *don't* got to *pee.* Why do you people always think that I've got to pee? Do I *look* like I got a bladder the size of a *quarter?* And by the way, peeing up here would be *nasty.*"

"Fine. Don't pee." Kaylee was already nostalgic for the crying, clinging Rosa. "Sit tight. Don't move. And if anyone else other than me or Ramon comes up on the other roof . . . "

Well. She didn't like entertaining that thought. What could Rosa do to protect herself, other than hide? "I'll push the ladder so it falls down," Rosa suggested. "That way they can't get to me. How's that sound? Is that a good idea?"

"Yes. A very good idea." Of course, if that happened, Kaylee and Ramon wouldn't have a way off the other roof . . . but, at that point, they'd have bigger problems on their hands. "You think you can remember that?"

With scorn, Rosa said, "I ain't *dumb*. Do you have to cross that ladder again?" When Kaylee nodded, Rosa said, "Don't you get scared?"

Good question. Scary as the ladder might be, it was nothing compared to what Kaylee was going to have to face once she was back inside the other building. She cleared her throat and tried to sound brave, for Rosa's sake. "Everybody gets scared. You've got to keep on going, though. One little rung at a time."

4:26 P.M.

Either Kaylee's imagination was running wild or the darkness in the garage building really was heavier and more dense than when she had left. On this journey, however, she had no hand to hold, nor any of Rosa's belongings to clutch as she made her way through the doorway and down the stairs. She moved alone through the darkness, careful not to make so much as the slightest of sounds, and its weight was more burden than she thought she could bear.

What kind of idiot willingly walked toward danger when she could easily run away? After all, Kaylee didn't owe either Ramon or his sister anything—the only thing Ramon had succeeded in doing in the last five hours was to get Kaylee further and further away from her goal. She could have somehow escaped from the rooftop and made her way home in what time she still had left, away from criminals, away from darkness, away from the Pastors. Yet here she was, smack in the middle of another sticky situation, without so much as a scrap of a plan.

Was that a noise? Kaylee stopped at the bottom of the stairs, her ears straining to hear anything over the incredibly loud pounding of her own heart. Even breathing deafened her, yet she couldn't stop gulping for air. Her lungs demanded oxygen, sending prickly white waves of need from chest to brain and into the tips of her fingers and toes. When she took a step forward, hand tracing the stairwell wall, placing her foot down slowly and carefully to make certain there was solid concrete ahead, she feared she wouldn't hear if she kicked something over and it clattered across . . .

Click. Kaylee froze, knowing in her motionlessness that whatever had triggered that noise, it hadn't been of her doing. That awful woman could be somewhere in the room with her. Maybe she had some kind of night vision goggles, like in the movies. Stolen, of course. The thought that someone could be watching her every move was paralyzing.

Yet that was a ridiculous idea. Right? Why would anyone stalk her in the darkness? Even if the woman knew how to operate night vision goggles—which was a pretty big *if*—why would she play a cat-and-mouse game when she could easily knock Kaylee over the head and dispose of her unconscious body? None of it made sense. The noise could have been anything, from the Grand Marquis's engine cooling off to the old building settling. She had to move forward despite her fear, in the same way she'd told Rosa: one step at a time.

She found a clear spot on the floor, let her foot connect, and inched ahead. Her fingertips traced the stair's cool metal frame for an instant before it sloped upward to the next floor. For a brief second she felt bristly concrete, and then her hand collided with something that leaned against the wall. Something softer, covered with cloth. Something warm and human.

A hand shot out of the dark and wrapped around her face, groping for her mouth before she could make a sound. Another strong arm grabbed her around her middle, yanking her backward.

"It's me," she heard a familiar voice whisper into her ear. "Don't say any—*oof!*" Kaylee's self-defense training took over. Her brain recognized Ramon's voice immediately, but her elbow had already begun swinging back and up into her attacker's rib cage. Her father would have been glad to know the move worked; Ramon staggered back, gagging, until Kaylee heard him thump against the stairwell.

Immediately she whirled around and fumbled in space until she found him crouched in a fetal position. *"Dios!"* he wheezed, his voice barely a whisper.

"I'm sorry!" Could anyone hear them? Was it safe to talk? She kept the volume low to apologize. "I tried to pull out of it at the last second. Are you okay? Ramon?"

He took a moment to answer. "I'll be good. Give me . . . " He wheezed. Kaylee had never taken a direct hit to the solar plexus, but she winced in sympathy. At the same time, she couldn't help but feel overjoyed at the fact that she'd found him alive and in one piece. Before she'd attacked him, anyway. "No reason for me to teach you how to make a fist, huh?"

"Did they hurt you?" Her whispered questions

started to fly. "Where are they? How did you get away?"

She sensed him moving; a finger pressed without warning against her lips. "Don't talk." As if punctuating his command, she heard a door slam in the distance, followed by the sounds of angry, quarreling voices. Though Ramon kept silent while he uncurled and stood erect, Kaylee could tell by the way he clutched at her hand for support that she'd elbowed him pretty thoroughly; he almost seemed to radiate waves of throbbing, peppery pain.

Once on his feet, he pulled her head close and whispered, his lips nuzzling through her thick hair to reach her ear, "They've been lookin' through some rooms over there. On the other side." The darkness simply felt better with him there to share it. His hand cupped her chin and opposite cheek as he spoke, warming a crescent of her skin. "Is Rosa—?"

Another door opened. The voices receded. It was Kaylee's turn to take Ramon's head in her hands and turn his ear toward her mouth. His mass of hair was silkier to the touch than she anticipated, like cool water between her fingers. "She's fine," she assured him in as low a whisper as she could produce. "Let's get the hell out of here."

"Not yet," he said, once they had switched positions again. "They'll follow if we don't get them off the track."

Once again, the voices resumed their quarrel, sounding angrier than before. Kaylee couldn't hear distinct words. Even with danger so close, how could she not regret the moment Ramon's hand left her face, even if it did drop to intertwine with her own fingers? He led her away from the wall, seeming to know where he was going. Her knee brushed against the Grand Marquis's bumper. They were moving toward the garage's center.

She had to warn him—the gaping service pit was probably mere feet away and the last thing she wanted at this point was to have him plunge down and kill himself. Yet the voices were coming closer. The most she could do was squeeze his fingers and try to drag him back. Ramon stopped. Before Kaylee could explain to him the danger ahead, she felt him let go of her hand and drop to the floor. He tugged on the fabric of her shorts; she knelt beside him.

". . . your fault we're in this mess," she heard a man's voice say.

". . . not taking any responsibility, and when Mr. C. finds out what you . . . threatening a kid like that . . . "

". . . always such a brown-noser, Angela. If you had been watching the door, that little punk wouldn't . . . "

They didn't bother to keep their words hushed. Forget night vision goggles—she didn't need them to locate the car thieves in the total blackness. She could have chucked lug wrenches and hit them right on their heads. If only she had one! Once again, Ramon reached for her hand and pulled her forward slightly, reaching out with it and patting it against where a projection of metal ran around a ledge of concrete. The service pit. They were mere inches away from it. What in the world did Ramon have in mind? They weren't going to go *down* there, were they? No. At least, not yet. He wanted to show her what was there, in case she didn't know. Ramon began to twist around, shifting positions. Kaylee felt a moment's anxiety at being overheard, but the couple's cursing drowned out any of the slight sounds he made.

"I wasn't *really* gonna hurt the little Spic. I was gonna lock him and the others up while we cleared out. We can't use this location anymore as it is now. Someone would've found them eventually."

"Maybe," said the woman. "Maybe not." To Kaylee, it sounded as if she didn't care either way. She shivered.

She felt Ramon's lips against her ear once more. "Hold my legs," he commanded.

What? Hold them why? Even when he grabbed her hands and planted them firmly on his shins, she didn't understand. She couldn't ask for an explanation, though. Not with their pursuers so close. Only a few minutes before she had asked Ramon's little sister to trust her; now she would have to return the favor. Funny how the universe so often worked out like that. Stupid universe.

Kaylee held tight to Ramon's legs as he adjusted himself to a lying-down position, wishing desperately that she knew what he had in mind. Why were the two of them simply sitting there when they should be on the move? Kaylee's every instinct was to run. Hadn't they run before? They'd fled the elevator when it started to act up. They'd escaped from Carl all day. Why weren't they running now? Ramon certainly didn't have a proven track record of success, by any means.

From the room's far end all hell seemed to break loose. It sounded like the world coming to an end, except with wheel covers as cause, rather than an asteroid or global warming. Aluminum rims seemed to be bouncing everywhere and rolling to a stop. One or two made it nearly as far as where Kaylee and Ramon waited in the dark. With every new clash and clatter, Kaylee's synesthesia conjured pale, jagged bolts of lightning that more than anything else made her want to let loose and run for the stairs. She couldn't let go, though. Not with Ramon lying so close to the gaping hole in the floor. She clung on, closed her eyes, and waited for it all to be done with. "Crap!" said the man, when most of the rolling discs had rattled to a stop. "Crap, crap, crappity crap crap!"

"Way to tell those kids where you are," commented the woman.

"Shut up, Angela." The sheer viciousness of the words made Kaylee shiver.

While the adults argued, Ramon's body began to shift. His legs began to slide from Kaylee; she increased her pressure, feeling bone beneath his muscle. What was he doing? Was he planning to trip them if they came to their section of the room? Without warning, Ramon's body grew heavy. While Kaylee's sweaty palms grappled to keep hold, she realized he'd leaned backward over the service pit, his knees bent at the edge. Yet she wasn't supporting his entire weight; she deduced that he must somehow be supporting himself as well with an arm. Right as she felt grateful she wasn't the only thing keeping Ramon from plunging headlong onto the sub-basement floor below, she felt his body jerk.

She clutched tighter. A moment later, from a distance and on the lower level, she heard something clatter. It sounded remarkably like someone kicking something down below. "Did you hear that?" the man asked, the volume of his voice for once dropping.

"That was from downstairs," said the woman.

Ramon was using the ancient trick of throwing something to distract their attention. Why weren't they moving, though? Did the thieves realize it was a hoax? Had Kaylee made some sound to give away their real location? Without warning, Ramon's whole body jerked again; she could imagine his hanging torso swinging in the space below from the motion. After a few seconds, another something banged to the floor. "The kid's down there," said the man. A second later, his voice muffled as if he'd turned away, he added, "Let's get him." When one of them stepped on something and sent it flying into the wall, he added with a growl, "Quietly!"

Kaylee didn't know where the stairs to the lower level were, but apparently they lay somewhere in the corner farthest away. Under cover of the racket the pair made when they kicked some of the aluminum hubcaps still littering the floor around their feet, Kaylee helped Ramon back up to a sitting position. He rocked alarmingly to one side, probably disoriented by the darkness and by hanging upside down for nearly a minute. Well, no wonder! He'd been an idiot, taking a risk like that!

She put her hands on his arms to steady him, still maintaining their silence. Side by side they sat, their legs pointing in opposite directions. With her hands on his biceps, she could feel his chest filling with air. Where her thumb brushed against the muscles of his chest, she could feel underneath the insistent, steady rhythm of his heart. In the dark, she had to rely on what senses were available to her. Her real senses, that is—the feel of his muscles, warm and velvety to the touch, though hard beneath. The sound of his breathing. The smell of his skin. She could see him in her mind; she imagined he was looking back at her through the mantle of blackness.

She wanted to complete the experience. Kaylee felt compelled to taste him once again. Leaning forward, their mouths met in midair. Had he felt the same desire as she? His lips seemed almost as hungry as hers when they pressed against each other. It was stupid to be kissing right at this moment when things were at their worst, but it seemed almost necessary. Being next to Ramon gave her hope; although she'd promised herself that the kiss in the car had been a one-time mistake, she'd been fooling herself. Hadn't she thought he'd been hot, the first time she'd looked at him? Why deny herself the possibility of a happy future when the present was the worst it had ever been?

The kiss lasted only a moment. When finally their faces separated, it was as imperceptibly as the moon's slow path across the sky. Kaylee felt slightly dizzy. Ramon's lips dragged across her cheek, his nose parting her hair until at last in her ear, he whispered, "We'd best go."

The words were a splash of cold water. She opened her eyes to find the garage still warm and dark, but silent now that their captors had vanished. When she turned her attention below, listening through the hole in the floor next to them, she thought she could hear quiet pursuit. "Yeah, okay." Once more she almost regretted the intimacy they'd shared seconds before. She was stupid to expect from Ramon . . . what? A compliment? A handshake? She shook the thoughts from her head. The kiss had been another moment's passing craziness.

With strong arms, he helped Kaylee to her feet. "I didn't want to leave through that door while they were nearby," he explained. "It's a little lighter on the other side, so if you're payin' attention, you can tell when it opens. That's how I knew you were comin' back down."

"They won't hear us?" she asked, trying to sound like everything was business as usual.

"Not if we stay quiet. You been up there . . . you lead."

They were quiet. And speedy, too, as they climbed the stairs and slipped through the doorway into the next stairwell. Kaylee would have felt safer if there'd been some sort of lock on the door's other side, but she would simply have to hope they had enough lead time to make it to the roof and over to the next building before the man and woman picked up their trail. After everything that had happened in the last hour, her steps felt tentative and shaky. Ramon, on the other hand, seemed positively gleeful at their escape; he took the stairs two or three at a time until they had both reached the top.

"Aw, man, this feels *good!*" he exulted once they were out in the sun and the door was shut tight behind them. In one swift motion he grabbed the neck of his sleeveless T-shirt and pulled it off, shaking his thick hair like a dog after a bath. Watching his naked torso emerge was like witnessing an already handsome caterpillar transform into a magnificent butterfly. Ramon's chest was lean and defined; his brown skin tightly hugged muscles in all the right places. A thin trail of hair led down from his chest to his navel, then down his flat stomach to disappear into his low-hanging shorts. Kaylee tried to avert her eyes. He was so fine that it almost hurt to look at him. "Where's Rosa?"

"What?" She sounded vague, caught up in the honeysuckle tendrils of his voice. "Oh. Don't freak." She pointed in the direction of the greenhouses and the wooden ladder spanning the ledges between their building and the next, grateful their avenue of escape was still there. "She's probably pooped. I told her to wait in the shade on the other side."

"You serious? You got her across that thing?" He sounded incredulous. "Rosa *hates* heights. I can't even barely get her to climb down the fire escape from George's after her lessons. You sure she crossed that?"

Kaylee grinned at Ramon's blatant admiration. It—and his shirtlessness—made her feel a little shy. "Ask her yourself." Feeling a little show-offy, she sprinted over to the ladder with him close behind. "Hold it for me while I go over."

She wasn't so cocky that she wanted to make any mistakes in the crossing, so she didn't linger or talk again until she was safely on the other side. "Your turn!"

"Dang, army princess! I can't do it like *that,*" he said, whistling. "But yeah. Okay. Only . . . hold. it steady. You know. Real firm."

Kaylee grinned at his obvious nervousness. He sat down on the ledge, swung his legs up, and crouched down at the ladder's other end, balancing. Ramon looked like a cat hiding in the bushes, spying on a squirrel while its rear end waggled in preparation to leap. She waited. The leap never came. "I've got the ladder," she said, in case he wasn't certain.

"Yeah." He stared right at her and beyond, keeping his eyes away from the ground. In the sun, his bare skin glistened with sweat. Suddenly he rose two inches into the air and sank back down again.

He'd been trying to psych himself up for the undertaking, she realized. "We've got to hurry," Kaylee reminded him. "Why don't you grab onto the ladder and—"

Ramon's response was short and irritable. "I don't need help."

"I'm trying—"

"I don't need your help!" he repeated.

Frustration gnawed at her nerves. She sounded snappish herself when she replied. "If you'd—"

"Shut up already, would ya!"

Even before she could process his reproach, the rational half of her mind started thinking up excuses for him. *He's scared. He doesn't mean it. People are grumpy when they're stressed out.* Was it the sun scorching her face right then, or the flames of her own anger? Kaylee couldn't tell. Why was he so *mean* all of a sudden, after they'd . . . well, down in the garage? She clamped shut her lips and watched as, like Rosa, he made a slow and steady path across the ladder, drawing closer and closer. What was she to Ramon? A pair of convenient lips to mack down on when he wanted, and someone to criticize the rest of the time? Only someone to tease for the afternoon?

Ramon didn't slip or fumble as he drew near— though some part of Kaylee wanted for a savage second to see him scared again. So he didn't like asking her for help? She bet his tune would change if he was hanging with white knuckles from one of the ladder's rungs, begging her to save him.

Oh, good God, Kaylee thought to herself. She was going crazy. Of all people, why in the world was she wishing Ramon harm? Because he'd snarled a little? As if she could complain, after all the whining she'd done over that stupid fire escape earlier! Kaylee wasn't used to having such strong feelings about people. Even when she and Carl had been caught cheating, she'd felt more numb and horrified at herself than angry at him. Today, though, it seemed like there were no moderate temperatures to her emotions—only frying pans at top temperature from which she leapt, one to the other, while her feelings sizzled like an egg cracked into hot grease.

"You're almost there," she told him, trying not to betray her ragged mood.

"Yeah, I know." Ramon sounded tense and uncertain.

They were both so *stupid.* She and Ramon were like third-graders who would tease each other and pinch or pull at the other's hair because they didn't have words grand enough to express how they really felt. Why couldn't she admit to herself that she liked him, and that her temper had flared because she wanted him to like her back? He was right in front of her now, his legs cramped and quivering. The T-shirt tucked into the back of his shorts swayed while he struggled to find a way to stand up without falling backward. His lips were pressed together in a tense line. So, he still wouldn't ask for help, would he?

Fine. She would give her help anyway. The big baby. One of her hands reached out to grab his waistband, her fingers snaking inside his shorts at the hip, while the other took hold of his wrist. Better to fall three feet than four stories. He took hold of her shoulders and leapt off the ladder so that its other end jumped up in the air and shuddered back down, askew. In their pose they studied each other for a few moments, faces too blank to betray any real sentiments. This face-off was entirely different from the closeness they'd shared in the dark. They could see each other plainly now— every pimple, every pore, every flaw. "We'd better take down the ladder," Kaylee murmured. She began to ease her fingers from his shorts, blushing when it took several seconds to untangle her thumb from the belt loop nearest his hip.

Ramon didn't let go. "Hey, I'm sorry," he said. The words dampened her angry flames. She nodded, not replying. "No, really." The boy raised his eyebrows. "It was kinda intense. Okay?"

Intense was right. "Yeah. It's okay." They let go of each other, slowly and reluctantly, and leaned out to pull the ladder over to their own side of the gap. By the time they leaned it on its side, out of sight against the ledge, Kaylee wore a small smile. "Can we please get out of here now?"

"Army princess, that's the exact thing I was gonna say. Hey, Rosa! Look who's here!" Ramon held up a hand to call across the roof while they jogged in the direction of the dilapidated greenhouse. "It's your big brother!"

Kaylee kept an eye on the other building's rooftop door. Once again, her sneakers were melting into the asphalt. "She probably doesn't want to come out of the sha . . . " Her words trailed off into silence. They halted.

Rosa wasn't behind the greenhouse. The lawn chair still sat where Kaylee had left it earlier, but of Rosa, her backpack, and her violin case, there was no trace.

Once again, Kaylee's heart began to thud against her ribs like a caged animal desperate for escape. What had she done? Where was Rosa? Had someone taken her? Why couldn't someone just kill her now? Even as her mind began to work out every calculation for disaster, her mouth moved. "Maybe . . . maybe she's in the greenhouse. I'll . . . "

Before she could take a step, Ramon grabbed Kaylee's wrist. "Listen." She strained her ears. It was a moment before they both heard the same thing—the sound of a violin in heart-wrenching melody.

They found Rosa on the floor below, sitting in a room by herself. Kaylee had never seen a building in such a decaying state. Broad curls of paint peeled from the ceiling and lay littered around the floor. Various people had over the years spray-painted the walls with graffiti. Half-burned old books spilled out of an antique fireplace, and the room smelled like cat urine and rot. And yet in the midst of the chaos and stifling heat sat Rosa on a crumbling wooden chair, instrument at her chin, producing the loveliest music Kaylee had ever heard. It would be a long time, she decided, before she heard something that unexpectedly beautiful again.

"Dang, girl, don't go scarin' your brother like that!" said Ramon.

The music halted. Rosa looked up, flashed her white teeth in a grin, and instantly leapt up to put away her violin. Finally she lunged at her brother. "You got out!"

"Well, yeah!" Ramon sounded as if his return was a given. "And what're you doin' down here when . . . "

Rosa already had her list of justifications ready. "It was *hot* up there. And the sun hurt my eyes. And my hiding place was a *lot* better than your girlfriend's." Her voice softened. "Are you okay?"

"Yeah, yeah, I'm cool," said Ramon, looking over his sister's head at Kaylee and giving her a wink. "But get your stuff. We gotta get goin' before those freaks catch up with us, okay?"

That was exactly what Kaylee wanted to hear. The faster they fled, the better. Rosa obediently went to collect her things. "I can find us another ride if you want," she volunteered.

"No!" said Kaylee and Ramon at once. Yeah, things felt okay again between them, Kaylee realized. The moment's awkwardness had passed.

"This time," Ramon said, jutting out his jaw with stubborn decision, "we *walk*."

5:40 P.M.

"You've got to be kidding me." Kaylee glared at Ramon, squatted down in front of a used bookstore on Park Avenue. A display of old *Life* magazines framed his head. "You're the one who's all buffed. You can't be tired."

Surrounded by smiling black-and-white snapshots of Marilyn Monroe and John F. Kennedy, Ramon looked miserable. His hands cradled his face like he worried his head might fall off. "I'm not tired," he said to the pavement. "Like I said, I need to get my second wind."

He was tired, though. They all were, although Park Avenue's gentle slope had been the easiest part of their walk so far. Rosa had surrendered her violin and backpack to Kaylee and Ramon a half hour before. Even unencumbered, she looked utterly beat . . . but still frisky compared to her brother. On the other hand, Kaylee's sneaker-clad feet were a little sore, but she was prepared to walk as far and as quickly as necessary. Every fresh glance at her wristwatch should have produced a new freak-out, but at this point the time issue was like an old bruise she'd poked and prodded too much. It no longer was such a sore point. "Okay," she said, resigning herself to the notion that they could all use a five-minute rest. "Let's relax a little."

Scarcely had she and Rosa slid to the ground than Ramon sprang up. "I told you, I don't gotta rest. I had to get my wind. That's all. Let's get goin'." Kaylee and Rosa exchanged an unconvinced glance and regained their feet.

Weaving back into the crowd wasn't as easy as stepping to the side had been. A mass exodus of Manhattan seemed to be taking place on foot that afternoon. What were those rats called, the ones that all blindly followed each other, even if it meant they threw themselves off a cliff into the ocean? Lemmings. That was it. This far downtown, the sidewalks were packed with lemmings strolling with a single direction in mind. "We ain't all nature girls like you, army princess," Ramon said. Kaylee didn't take offense. His tone was generous and friendly, and it really did sound as if he'd gotten that second wind.

"Yeah, but you're all, you know. Muscley." She flushed slightly at the memory. Ramon had put his shirt back on a long while ago, but the still visible sweet curves of his biceps reminded her of what she'd seen of the rest of him.

"That's liftin' weights and some b-ball," Ramon said. "It's not the endurance kind of stuff you do. Hey, Rosa, know what I thought the first time I saw Kaylee?"

Rosa's mouth snapped open so quickly that Kaylee braced herself for the slander that was sure to follow. Since their rooftop escapade, though, Rosa had been curiously unwilling to bad-mouth her brother's friend. Her lips twitched to the side, muffling whatever smart-mouthed remark she'd dreamed up. "What?" she finally asked.

"I thought she was like, this rich chick with an attitude. Stuck up. Real trouble." While Ramon spoke, Kaylee thought back to those first few minutes in the elevator. Was it really only earlier today? It felt like weeks ago. The notion that Ramon had thought her stuck up when she'd been scared and angry embarrassed her. On the other hand, she remembered that she herself had thought Ramon was probably a thug . . . and real trouble as well. "But then she started bustin' out all these crazy skills. Climbin', runnin', scamperin' across a ladder like a monkey. Who knew?" He tried to grin in her direction, but he was so worn out, the smile barely registered. He must have noticed her look of pity, because he cocked his head and admitted, "Okay, maybe I am a little tired after all."

For the fortieth time in as many minutes, Kaylee felt guilty. "Let's try to flag down a car or something." There were enough of them crowding the streets, moving at a slow pace.

"Nah." Ramon began limping forward again, Rosa bringing up their rear. "We gotta get you back before seven. It'll just be wastin' time."

"But your feet are hurting. And Rosa's whipped." Rosa didn't bother to confirm or deny the charge. "Lis-

ten, I'm sorry we ran into a little trouble with that Angela woman, but . . . "

"Big trouble," said Ramon.

"Big trouble. I'm sorry we went through it, I really
am, mostly for . . . " Kaylee looked back over her
shoulder and held out a hand to the little girl trailing
behind. Surprisingly enough, Rosa accepted it.
"Mostly for Rosa's sake."

"I keep tellin' you, it wasn't your fault."

"But it was!" How could she make him understand? It was tough enough admitting blame to herself, much less to someone whose good opinion she
cared about. "I had this feeling . . . "

"Whoa, hold up." Tired he might have been, but
Ramon had strength enough to pull Kaylee from the
stream of pedestrians and into an office building's
empty entryway. Despite the talk of passersby, the
sound of traffic, and the whistles of policemen direct-
ing traffic, the little portico felt like a haven of peace.
Rosa took the opportunity to retrieve and sit on her violin case, too weary to join the conversation. "You had
a feeling? You mean with your extra sense?"

"It's not—never mind." She didn't want to have to
explain her condition again. "Yeah, and I didn't say
anything."

"What'd you feel?"

"Well, remember that guy on the street, the easy-
peasy-Japanesey guy? When he was creeping me out,
he kind of tasted . . . oily."

That was enough to rouse Rosa. "You was *licking*
some guy on the street? Ew! Nasty!"

Kaylee ignored her. "And sometimes when people talk, I smell stuff. With her, it was kind of a weird, peppery . . . "

"You were sniffin' in the car!" Ramon pointed a finger at her. He was angry, after all. "And you said it was something weird you smelled."

"Don't be mad!"

"I'm not mad!" Ramon seemed genuinely surprised that she'd suggested such a thing. "But I keep tellin' you, you got this . . . "

She thought she knew what he was going to say. "I'm not psychic!"

"No, you're right." That admission left her jaw hanging open. "But you know, the brain works at, like, a zillion miles a second. It's takin' in all this information through the eyes, the ears, from what your skin and muscles are feelin', and it's sendin' back directions to all these places. Bam! Bam! Bam! Shootin' off electricity through synapses like crazy." His hands had become animated, illustrating the brain's activity with a series of punches and claps. "And your body is reactin' to stuff before you know what's goin' on. So like, the lights are goin' out, your ears hear it and your eyes catch it happening and bam! Bam! Your mouth's all juicy before your head starts thinkin', *Hey, the lights are goin' out.* Right?" She nodded, waiting to hear what he had to say next. "So, like, with that woman, your brain's pickin' up all kinds of things that you're not really *noticing.* Like, maybe you saw the seat was too far back for her, or that she looked all nervous and stuff. All these little signs, right, that something's up.

161

You're not thinkin' to yourself, *Oh hey, this woman's jackin' this car.* But your brain's like, *Hello, army princess! Pay attention!"*

"Yes," she said. She'd never thought of her condition like that. He was making perfect sense.

"So like, for me, I get this feelin' in my stomach that somethin's not right. And you, because you're special, you get . . . "

"The smell," Kaylee finished. "I get smells. And colors, and feelings on my skin." Light was dawning. In the street, she'd seen Carl in color and the rest of the world in gray not because of any psychic ability, but only because her brain was trying to draw attention to what it had noticed.

"But hey—" He stepped forward and took her hands in his. "It's not your fault! I got that feelin' in my stomach that lady wasn't right before we got in the car. You got a smell. We shoulda listened to, you know, our instincts, instead of being so hot to get out of there that we did the wrong thing. Right?"

She nodded. Having someone actually *understand* her, and even to be able to explain Kaylee to herself was . . . well, she'd never experienced anything like it. The feeling was better than opening the best present beneath the Christmas tree. "Thank you." Kaylee colored at the sight of his sideways grin.

"Okay, so tell me: You taste somethin' when you hear me talk? Or what? You smell somethin'? Is that it?" She'd blushed more deeply at the question, probably obviously enough that he noticed. "You smell somethin'! What do you smell?"

"Armpit sweat and canned Spam," she told him,

too embarrassed to admit the truth. Even now, his ten-drils of honeysuckle snaked forward to attach themselves. "How come you know all that stuff about synapses? You're smarter than you look."

He had worn a happy and excited expression, but at her last statement, Ramon's face fell. Oh crap. She'd said the totally wrong thing. "No, I don't mean . . . "

"I know what you meant," he said, drawing into himself.

Damn it! How could she have been so stupid? She might as well have climbed in a car, pulled the door shut, and stared at Ramon through the glass while her hands slammed closed the lock, merely because of the clothes he wore and the color of his skin. "No, don't be stu—silly." Her mouth fumbled for the right words. Safe words. "I mean, you said a minute ago that I was full of surprises, right? Monkey girl? It's that you're—you're the same way. Full of surprises. I like that about you, Ramon!"

The hard look on his face softened a little. After a moment, he nodded. "I got my wind back. Let's walk some more. You ready to move, *princesa?*"

Rosa seemed none too happy, but she stood up, shook out her thick hair, and nodded.

When Ramon grabbed for his sister's violin case, Kaylee tried to beat him to it. "You've already got the knapsack," she told him. "Let me."

"I'll be okay." Ramon's voice was still thawing, cold from her slip of the tongue. "Let's get goin'."

They walked in silence for two blocks, passing black and empty stores, office buildings, and restaurants. One of the businessmen in front of Kaylee had already removed his jacket and slung it over his shoulder while he stumbled forward, the back of his shirt soaked with sweat. She was feeling none too fresh at this point, either, and judging by the way her mouth couldn't control what was coming out of it, her brain could have use a good cool shower as well. At least the buildings were blocking out the late afternoon sun. "So what's gonna happen after we get you home?" Ramon finally asked, breaking the silence between them.

"You mean, like with school?" His question had surprised her.

"I mean, like with you and me." Ramon wasn't looking at her now. She'd completely screwed up things. When they got to the river, she planned to jump in it.

"Listen, Ramon, when I said what I said a minute ago . . . "

"This isn't about that," he said insistently. "Am I gonna be able to, like, see you again?"

"Yes!" she told him, anxiety cascading from her like water over a fall. Was that all this was about? "I'd like to. Yes!"

" 'Cause I want to see you again, too."

"Oh, man," she heard Rosa say with distaste from behind them. "At least the blackout isn't makin' me miss the soaps."

"¡Callate!" growled Ramon. He turned to Kaylee. "So, okay. We get you home before your dad's back at seven. Then I want to see you sometime. What're you gonna tell your mom and pop about me?"

Maybe the boy's brain worked more quickly than her own; she couldn't tell at all where he was going with these questions. Kaylee didn't even know how to answer. "Well, I mean . . . I'd have to make something up about how we met, because I couldn't tell them . . . what?" He stared stubbornly at the rear of a largish woman in front of him, apparently angry once again. "What? It's more convenient!"

"You don't think I'm good enough."

"That's not true." It felt like they were back to square one again, stuck in the elevator with him thinking she was stuck up and her convinced he was stupid and dangerous. She hated it. They'd traveled so far since being trapped in that box!

"Start with one lie and you'll be tellin' tales about me all the time," Ramon said, as quietly as he could considering the city's noise.

"So you want me to what, tell my dad where I've really been all day?" Her own anger began to build, tasting like salted lemons. "Because when I'm sent away to military school and grounded until my mid-twenties, you're not going to be able to see me at all. You realize that?"

"How'm I gonna know whether you tell them about me at all?" he countered. "I ain't nothin' to boast about. What if you too proud to tell them? What if it's more *convenient* to tell them you're goin' out to meet Muffy and Buffy and Tiffany at the mall instead of tellin' them you're meetin' Rico Suave? What about that, huh?" Before she could think up an answer, he added, "This ain't no *West Side Story*. I ain't gonna be Tony."

"Tony was the *white* boy," Rosa informed him flatly. "Maria . . . "

"Whatever. The priest says there's such a thing as a lie of omission. Leavin' out truth from what you say is as bad as lyin', you know."

"I know what a lie of omission is! Ramon, I . . . " Every sense in the world couldn't help her read the boy; X-ray vision wouldn't even do the trick. Kaylee struggled for words. "I thought we were friends. I thought we were *more* than—I wouldn't do that!"

"Yeah. So you say."

"Besides, you've got your own lies of omission," she snapped back. "What about Manuel?"

"What about Manuel?" Ramon sounded defensive. His shoulders tensed.

"There's been this whole issue going on today about you and him. You think *I'm* proud? How about you being too proud to let him into your life?"

"That ain't none of your business."

"He could help Rosa get into that school. All you have to do is ask."

The boy seemed to grow more sullen and withdrawn. "That's family business. Okay?" He halted, then stumbled forward again. "I know you got a point. But it ain't a hammer and you don't gotta keep poundin' away at me."

"I'm not—that's totally unfair! I don't want to . . . ! Just forget I said it." She didn't know why they were having this discussion. Or was it a fight? Their voices weren't raised, but it felt as if thunderclouds hovered over both their heads, ready to unleash furies without warning. Ahead of them, Park Avenue bordered a moderate expanse of trees intersected by concrete. They must have reached Union Square. A couple of blocks farther, the street shot away in a diagonal that would lead them to the Manhattan Bridge. Hundreds upon hundreds of people were already walking in that direction.

A policeman issued shrill commands with the silver whistle protruding from his mouth, gesturing for the stream of people to cross over. They followed the crowd over to the park, where too many people to count milled around. The hubbub felt like constant needles across the back of Kaylee's neck, but she was so used to the sensation by now that all she could do was rub at it and her sore muscles. Some groups were obviously making a party of the event, spreading blankets over the shaded areas and cracking open coolers of beer and soda and tossing Frisbees to their dogs. Three policemen in vests answered questions for ten times as many people crowding around. There was too much activity going on for Kaylee to take it all in, especially with her head still spinning from the argument.

"Water?" Someone proffered a bottle right under her nose—a cheerful young woman on some sort of bicycle-propelled cart. The plastic bottle was covered with condensation and awoke a need that Kaylee had tried to ignore for hours. She didn't have much in the way of money, though. "It's free!" said the woman, waggling the gift. Had she been psychic? No, probably the look of disappointment on her face had been plain enough to read. "Courtesy of the Chelsea Food Co-op. We're trying to help out stranded commuters. And kids who look thirsty!" She grinned.

"Thanks!" She hesitated, wanting to chug the water instantly but not wanting to keep it from the Pastors. Maybe the three of them could share? No need. The woman had dipped into her cart and given both the Pastors bottles of their own before pedaling off with a peal of her bell. Rosa immediately began to glug down huge swigs from hers; Ramon wasn't far behind in his attempt to rehydrate. As for Kaylee, well, nothing had ever tasted so sweet. "That was lucky, huh?" she asked the other two, once she'd let the cool liquid wet her mouth and gullet.

"Man!" Ramon's spirits seemed revived once he reached the bottom of his bottle. Some of the water overflowed from the corners of his mouth and trickled down his neck, where it was absorbed by his shirt's grimy hem. "That's good! Drink up, *princesa.*"

Rosa had consumed about a third of her ration. She primly screwed on the cap and tucked the bottle into her pack. "I'm saving," she explained. "Besides, I know you're gonna take it from me and drink it later."

"I'm glad you feel better." It was a risk, but Kaylee wanted to say something to Ramon to make up for their . . . fight or misunderstanding or weirdness, or whatever it had been.

He shrugged. "Yeah. Okay." Ramon was still giving Kaylee the cold shoulder. It ached. How could anyone whose words smelled so sweet *hurt* her like that? She bit her lip and turned her attention to the water, letting it quench the furnace flaming within.

From behind them, Rosa laughed. When they turned to look at her, she laughed again and squinted in a sheepish way. Ramon raised an eyebrow. "It's funny," she said. " 'Cause after everyone makin' me pretend all afternoon, now I really gotta go." When neither of them responded, she repeated, "I *said*, I gotta *pee!*"

"I don't mind taking her," Kaylee said. There had to be something around here. A Porta-Potty, if not the real thing.

"Nah, I got it." Ramon looked around the park, peering through the crowds of rollerbladers and locals looking for shade, and lost men and women making their way home. He started to walk, gesturing for his sister to follow.

"No, really, I don't mind." Kaylee scampered to follow. As they passed the men and women still badgering the policemen with their questions, over the babble of voices, Kaylee heard one in particular that stood out from the rest—a man's, both bossy and slightly condescending. She recognized it immediately, but it took a minute to match her memory of it with the little man jumping up and down at the back of the cluster, trying to out-shout the others. She tugged the back of Ramon's shirt. "Look," she said, pointing. "It's Mr. Cloutier."

"Who?" Ramon asked, turning. Rosa thudded to a stop as well. "No kiddin'! Hey there, new papa!" He clapped the little businessman on his back.

Mr. Cloutier stopped bouncing on his toes. He whipped around and looked at them without recognition. "Do I know you?" he finally asked.

Ramon, in the meantime, seemed positively thrilled to see the man. When he spoke, Kaylee immediately understood why. "You just got here? Man, we didn't really lose much time then, did we? Hey, man!" He grabbed the little man's hand in a soulful shake. "How's Brody junior, bro?"

"How do you know my name?" The little man seemed dazed. Kaylee noticed that he looked none too put-together, either. Half of his shirt collar stood straight up. His coat and tie had vanished completely, and his shirt was dirty and open halfway to his navel, exposing a scoop-necked T-shirt underneath. In fact, he looked a bit as if he'd been tossed into a Dumpster and had to claw his way out. He squinted. "Oh, wait. You're those kids from my office building."

Ramon grinned and shook the little man's hand so that Mr. Cloutier's body shimmied like a dog's rubber toy. The older Pastor really was happy that their detours hadn't lost them any time. "Are you okay?" Kaylee asked. "Did you get . . . mugged?"

Mr. Cloutier self-consciously lifted a hand to his head, where he tried to smooth down his messed-up hair. "No. Why does everyone keep asking me that?"

"You still haven't gotten to your wife?" Kaylee wanted to know. He shook his head. Weird and pushy as the guy was, it was hard not to feel sorry about the look of obsession in his eyes.

"Dang!" said Ramon. "What hospital is she at?"

"NYU Downtown." Mr. Cloutier gulped. "That's where she called me from, before the lights went out."

"Oh, kinda down Wall Street, huh?" For an answer, the man's shoulders rose and fell in a sigh.

"In case you didn't hear me the *first* time," Rosa announced, beginning to dance with impatience, "*I gotta pee.*"

"Okay, okay." Ramon took her hand. "Be seein' you, man. You'll get there."

"Now!"

"Yeah," said Kaylee. She didn't want the Pastors to leave her behind. "Good luck."

Their wishes barely seemed to register. Mr. Cloutier sagged and turned, once again trying to catch the policeman's attention. Over her shoulder, Kaylee could tell he'd lost the heart for it. "That's sad," she said. "I bet his wife is crazy to know where he is, too."

"Yeah. At least he ain't ashamed of wantin' to be with her."

Ramon hadn't looked sideways in her direction when he delivered the sharp verbal slap. Striking back was pure instinct. "Maybe he'd be there by now if he hadn't been too proud to ask for help," she said, barely able to control her fury.

Ramon stopped then, turning around to face her. "You know, why don't you stay here a while," he told Kaylee. "Rosa's gotta pee, and I think you and me could use a couple of minutes apart."

"Yeah, you know, I think that's a fan-*tas*-tic idea." In fact, Kaylee couldn't think of anything else she'd rather do than spend a little bit of quality time with the one person in Manhattan who wouldn't argue with every little damned thing she said . . . herself. She squelched the impulse to look at her watch when she added, "Take your time. No rush."

"Sounds good to me. Come on, *princesa.*" When they walked away, Ramon whistled a careless tune. It wasn't until they were out of earshot that Kaylee recognized it as the Lemley concerto.

What an arrogant butthead he could be! Things had almost been simpler when the one thing keeping them together had been their original deal. The deal had been simple economics, a transaction they could both understand. Now their relationship was biology and sociology and psychology and a bunch of other -ologies, what with the kissing and the emotions she had for him . . . but what did she feel? Did he feel anything back? If he did, why was he being so prickly and obstinate?

Maybe his stubbornness came from his sentiments for her. Or maybe he was just an arrogant, macho, thick-headed *boy.* Why wasn't anything having to do with boys easy?

You know, Kaylee thought, she'd been totally wrong a minute ago. She did argue with herself over every little damned thing. "Water?" asked someone passing by. Kaylee tried to smile, showing her unfinished bottle. She could have downed four or five, but she didn't want to be greedy. What she really needed was a bottle of brain shampoo. Did anyone have any of that?

To distract herself, she began strolling around, not straying far from the broad expanse of concrete. From behind she heard the bicycle bell of one of the co-op water angels; on a bench nearby, a young black man unscrewed a bottle cap for an elderly white woman. A tiny little blond girl of no more than four or five raced in front of her, a pointy cap made of folded newspaper on her head. A woman scooped up the toddler, the pair of them laughing and seemingly carefree.

It was funny, wasn't it, how adaptable people seemed to hard times? A few hours ago, outside the office building where Mr. Cloutier worked, there had been nothing but worry and fear and voices raised in anger. Here it was, only a few hours later, and everyone in Union Square was behaving . . . well, calmly. There were still a few strident voices coming from that cluster around the policemen they'd passed, but by and large, everyone seemed almost serene. Among the stream of people making their way toward Fourth Avenue and the bridges, a kind of resignation seemed to prevail. Here in the park, there was laughter and the relaxed feeling of a Sunday afternoon picnic. People were helping each other. After an afternoon spent seeing the worst sides of human nature, the whole thing felt a little surreal.

A hand fell on her shoulder, freckled with age. "Are you lost?" said an older woman with her long gray hair pulled into a ponytail. She carried a clipboard and a walkie-talkie on her well-dressed hip. Kaylee smiled, came to herself, and shook her head. Didn't these people have places to be? It was all very nice and Sunday-school-lessony to talk about helping people, but she never realized that in times of trouble, people really *did* anything about it. The woman, however, didn't give up. She reminded Kaylee of one of the counselors she had to see after she was expelled—the type who never believed anything you said, even if you told them the world was round. "If you're separated from your parents, we've got a radio network set up at the park's south end," she said kindly.

"No, my dad's at work and my mom's in . . . well, out of town," Kaylee told her, trying to move on. "I'm trying to get home. Thanks tho . . . "

"Are you looking for a bus?" Kaylee startled right out of her skin at the question. "There are still a few buses leaving for the outlying areas."

A bus? She'd love a bus! Buses had comfy seats. Buses had air conditioning. Buses zoomed down streets and didn't require any walking, save to get on and off. "To Brooklyn?" she asked hopefully.

"Oh, no, to Connecticut and New Jersey, mostly," she said, dashing Kaylee's hopes before they grew too high. "But oh, there's—follow me?" She turned and with brisk steps began to walk down the concrete avenue.

Maybe it was her military upbringing that made her instantly respect someone of obvious authority, but Kaylee couldn't help herself. She followed obediently, grateful for once that afternoon to follow someone who knew what she was doing. "Have you heard anything about what caused the blackout?" she asked. "We—I haven't been near a radio all afternoon."

"They're saying it was an overload of a lot of interconnected electrical systems on a very hot day," the woman smiled back, turning and leading Kaylee in the direction of a cluster of people in the Square's center. "On the news they said we probably won't have power again until tomorrow or even the day after, because it's spread out over so many states and . . . oh, there she is. Layla?" she called out as Kaylee's sore feet attempted to catch up. There went any chances of the quick solution for which she'd been hoping all afternoon. "Layla? Do we have anyone going to Brooklyn?"

A younger blond woman turned around, her smiling face like a squat pumpkin's. Her hair spiked out all over her head in irregular tufts. She carried a clipboard similar to the older woman's. "Brooklyn?" she repeated.

What was going on here? After an afternoon's chaos, the army princess inside her hungered for order. The sight of organized people with clipboards invigorated Kaylee like no shower or hot bath ever could. "Are you serious?" she asked. "What's going on?"

"Volunteer ride shares," said the older woman. "Folks with space in their cars are transporting other people who need—I'm sorry, Layla, what?"

The young blonde had been waving her hand. "I think he's—sir? Sir? Did you say you were going to Brooklyn?"

"I am," thundered a deep voice behind Kaylee. "To Coney Island, but I don't mind making other stops. I was about to leave."

Oh, by all that was holy. There was hope. It was after six, and if the voice's owner really had a car, even in the slow traffic she could get home before her father. "I'm right at . . . "

Kaylee had been about to divulge her crossroads when she found herself staring at a belly. Not just any belly—an enormous belly about to burst from the constraints of a white tank top. Above it sagged two man-breasts. The shirt bulged like two hundred pounds of raw beef stuffed into a fifty-pound sack.

Then there were the arms—tattooed from the wrists all the way up to the shoulders, the ink spilling over the man's shoulders and chest. Even his neck and face had been tattooed, Kaylee realized in horror. A dragon curled around the man's cheek, its head flaming curlicues of fire over his eyebrows. Thick, curly hair fell down around the man's ears and cheeks; a rope of it had been pulled back, samurai-style, at the back of his head. This was definitely not the kind of stranger she should be riding in a car with. At Kaylee's slow glance up he bared his teeth, all of them equally yellowed save for one gold incisor. "Hi there, friend!" he boomed. "Henrique the Freak at your service."

He was smiling, she realized. She tried to lift up the corners of her mouth in return. When he spoke he smelled like . . . what scent was it? "Wow," she found herself saying.

"Wow?"

"Um, sorry," she replied. "You've really got a lot of tattoos. Not that there's anything wrong with them. My folks are in the military, so I see a lot of ink."

His eyes flickered down to her shirt. After reading the legend emblazoned there, he nodded. "So, do I scare you? My girl tells me I scare people. She's about your age. Professional hazard—I work a sideshow. You should come see my act sometime! I eat light bulbs!" Was that supposed to be an enticement?

"I'll let you two talk," said the smiling woman. "Good luck!" she told them before moving off.

Who wouldn't be scared by a freaky-looking light bulb–eater? But no, Kaylee thought to herself, stopping suddenly. Maybe she shouldn't listen to her fears.

What did her senses tell her? What scent did his words carry?

She recognized it from her childhood, when her mother used to bake . . . peanut butter cookies. That was exactly it. When he spoke, her nostrils were filled with the aroma of peanut butter cookies. Kaylee willed herself to ignore the man's off-putting exterior and follow what her instincts told her. "Nah," she said, grinning genuinely. "It's pretty cool, actually. So are you seriously going to Brooklyn? You can take me?"

"I've got my daughter and three suits in the back. If you wanna see scared, you should see those guys," he said with a hearty laugh. "If you don't mind squeezing in the front with my girl, there's room for you."

"But I'm in a group of three," she said, bitterly disappointed. She couldn't see herself, Ramon, and Rosa squeezing into a car already carrying five people, even with Rosa on someone's lap.

The man shrugged. "I've got room for only one, little lady," he said. "It could be you."

It could be her. In less than five minutes she could be sitting down in a car on her way home, driven to her door by Henrique the Freak. She'd probably have time for a shower when she got there. She could be out of Manhattan and away from Ramon. He'd never have to know why she went. The way he'd behaved in the last hour, she wasn't entirely certain he deserved to. All she had to do was nod her head to Henrique and they'd be on their way. Chances were that Ramon would forget about her by tomorrow, and any regrets she'd have . . . well, they'd vanish, too, along with the whole nightmarish day, when the lights came back on.

"Well?" said Henrique.

She looked up at him, knowing that she already had her answer. If she refused, she'd never get home before seven. "I'll take that space in your car, but can you do me a favor?" she begged, and explained what she needed. To her relief, he nodded. "Give me two minutes. Two minutes. I'll be right back," she promised, once again feeling something close to happy.

Only a fool would have turned him down.

Five minutes later, Kaylee had her eyes closed, her relaxed muscles enjoying the cool breeze that ran over her face and hair as she leaned back on the seat she'd chosen. Her decision had been right, she knew. This was exactly where she wanted to be. She felt a hand on her shoulder. "Hey," said a familiar voice.

She opened her eyes and found Ramon standing over the spot where she sat enjoying her shaded park bench. Rosa stood at his side. Both of them looked as refreshed as she felt. "Hey!" she exclaimed to both of them, standing once again on her sore feet.

"Sorry if we were gone a while. Kind of a long line."

"They were givin' away ice cream at the other end of the park," Rosa said, holding out a cup. "It's kind of melty. But I brought you some."

Kaylee felt kind of melty herself. "Aw, honey!"

"Don't get girly. Ramon *made* me," Rosa qualified.

"We miss anything?" Ramon wanted to know.

"Nah," she said. "Well, kind of. I found a guy willing to drive Mr. Cloutier to that hospital."

"Downtown Hospital?" Ramon said. "Seriously? Hey, that was pretty cool of you."

It wasn't the kind of thing that Kaylee could agree to without sounding conceited, so she shrugged. Neither of the Pastors needed to know about the temptation she'd faced. Not when they'd brought her ice cream. She popped off the top of the little pint and stirred her spoon around its melting contents, satisfied. "Yeah. I'm glad someone gets a happy ending. Let's walk," she suggested, pointing them in the direction of Fourth Avenue.

Not until they were at the edge of Union Square did Ramon speak again. "Hey," he said, his voice husky. "About happy endings. I've been thinkin' about this. I'm worried you're not gonna get home before seven, and I didn't want you believin' it's 'cause I was tryin' to get you in trouble with your old man or nothin' like that, so . . . "

"So I'm in trouble," Kaylee interrupted, knowing she meant what she was about to say. "Listen. I've been neck-deep all day and I survived. So did you."

"Yeah, but . . . " His eyes narrowed as they waited for another policeman to hurry them across the street. "You think we can make it?"

Kaylee tossed the container of ice cream into a garbage receptacle and grabbed Ramon's hand. "We won't know until we try."

Maybe she was a fool, but at least she'd end the day an honest fool. The policeman blew his whistle, and from the corner the pedestrians broke into the street like runners at the starting line, racing for the other side of the street and the bridge and river waiting beyond: She and Ramon kept their hands clasped and began the marathon home.

7:22 P.M.

One thing was certain: Tomorrow, Kaylee was going to have one very bad case of sunburn. Now that the sun's decline cast long shadows over the streets, the back of her neck was aflame with fiery prickles that she knew would soon be painful to the touch. Even stray strands of hair that brushed her cheeks made her wince. Yet she didn't complain. What would be the point? Everything hurt—her feet, her head, her skin, her joints.

Her heart.

At the street's end she paused. She knew these street signs, these houses, the kids' bicycles that had been left on the sidewalks. Kaylee should have been glad. Her feet should have been quickening their pace to shorten the distance between herself and everything that was recognizable in her life. She felt leaden, though, weighed down too heavily to continue. "What's the deal? Are we *there* yet?" Rosa's demands sounded lifeless, as if all she wanted was a nap. As if to confirm that impression, a mouth-stretching yawn punctuated the end of her question.

"It's there," Kaylee said, pointing to the third house from the corner, covered by the familiar old olive-green aluminum siding. She bent over and leaned on her knees, almost not willing to walk any farther. "We're here."

"About godda . . . " Ramon wasn't too tired to give Rosa a look designed to halt the profanity. "Well, isn't that peachy-keen," she said, changing over to the most sarcastic-sounding version of her little lady voice. "So let's drop off her *swell* butt at her *golly-nifty* house and get *home,* gee golly whillikers. We gotta walk another ten miles!"

"Rosa." Ramon spoke to his sister, but his eyes were squarely on Kaylee, "our place is less than half a mile from here. *Callate.*" To Kaylee he said in a soft voice, "I didn't realize you and me was so close."

She startled. What did he mean by that? Oh. Distance. She was so tired her mind couldn't take two and two and make them into four. Kaylee groaned. Thinking of mathematics only reminded her of the test she'd skipped that morning. "Yeah, me neither." How lame did that sound? She wished she had something better to tell him. She couldn't think of anything. "Let's get going." Kaylee shrugged and dragged herself to a standing position once more. "Get it over with."

"Should Rosa and me . . . ?"

Kaylee couldn't answer his question until she saw whether or not her father's Jeep was in the drive. It was still possible he might not be home yet, held up either by work or blackout-related traffic. She was too worn out from miles and miles of walking to feel terrified at the answer at this point. In her head she'd trod through this scenario so many times that she'd worn through her mental linoleum. If the Jeep was there, fine. The question of whether or not she'd be discovered would be answered for her, no effort involved. If it wasn't—well, she'd have to see.

Mrs. Scott, her next-door neighbor, waved at her from the front porch, where she and her husband sat in rocking chairs with Japanese fans in their hands. Kaylee could feel their eyes watching the Pastors as they followed. Suspicious, probably. Judging. She didn't bother to look back. Her own eyes were preoccupied with scanning up the concrete expanse of drive as she drew closer to home. A few more steps around the Scotts' hedge and she'd discover her fate.

The Glasses' driveway was empty, its gate wide open. Kaylee's father wasn't home.

For a few moments she couldn't believe what she saw—or didn't see. She'd made it home before her father. She was a few feet away from a house that at several points in the last few hours she'd despaired of seeing ever again. Even as burned out and dog-tired as she was, the realization that she'd actually *accomplished* what she'd set out to do sent chills up her spine. She'd done it. She'd run the course, obstacle by obstacle, and reached the finish line.

"So." When she turned, Ramon stood behind her, tall and lanky, still carrying his sister's violin. His eyes were shadowed by the oak branches overhanging the sidewalk. "I guess you did it," he said, echoing her own thoughts.

"I guess I did." They stared at each other in silence for a moment more until she said, "Ramon . . . "

"Listen . . . " he said at the same time.

They couldn't do this, not here in front of the house, with the Scotts listening in. She gestured for them to follow her up the drive and into the backyard. Ramon followed, looking around as if expecting Kaylee's father to jump out at any moment. Rosa simply took long and dramatically exaggerated steps. "I don't want this to be a good-bye." The words were out of her mouth scarcely before they'd turned the corner. Numb as she was from all the walking, the realization that she might never again see Ramon Pastor aroused jagged, fresh pain along every nerve ending in her body. "Please," she begged. "Not good-bye."

"Oh, *man*," groaned Rosa. "Here we go!"

Ramon ignored his sister. "Me neither, Kaylee. I don't want . . . " He leaned in, his lips searching for hers. "We been through too much."

"I'm scared," she said, resisting the temptation of his mouth. "Please . . . "

"What in heck you got to be scared about?" His lips curved into a smile, drawing closer and closer. "You? You're not an army princess. You're a freakin' army quee—"

Rosa's shriek fell on Kaylee's eardrums like a poison-edged dagger; Kaylee fell backward against the garden hose, shoved by some unknown and mighty force, but not before Ramon's jaw cracked into her forehead. For a moment she saw blackness, and then a pyrotechnic explosion of red and white. When she opened her eyes again, the taste of burnt leather lingered on her tongue. Carl stood before her, a nasty smirk on his face as he pivoted. Rosa's violin case hung from his hand, transformed from a battered thing of beauty to a battering weapon.

"What—?" Kaylee's brow throbbed, but Ramon lay on his side on the pavement, clutching the back of his head. Tears flowed from the corners of his eyes as he writhed in pain. Carl had nearly cracked his skull open!

"Feel good, huh?" Carl licked his lips and danced around, smug and satisfied with himself. "Play cat-and-mouse with me all day and you pay the price, *muchacho.*"

"My violin!" Kaylee didn't know what Carl had done to Rosa, but it had been enough to land her in the patch of grass near the potting shed. "Give it *back,* you big *butt!*"

"Shut up," Carl barked.

"It cost us a *lot of money!*"

"Well, little Kaylee here owes me a lot of money. Don't ya, Kaylee?"

She wiped her face and found blood. Ramon's, most likely. A thin stream of it still flowed from the corner of his mouth. "I owe you nothing."

"Oh, I think you do," Carl said, advancing on her. His teeth ground audibly.

"Kaylee." Ramon's mouth moved as if it hurt. He raised a hand to see if his jaw was still there, able only to squeeze out one word. "Run."

They could escape, Kaylee realized. She could grab Rosa and run to the Scotts for help. Yet she couldn't leave Ramon at the other boy's mercy, sprawled out and dazed from the blow. "No," she said. What was that chemical pumping through her chest? Adrenaline? Some synthesized chemical produced by her brain? No matter—it felt like courage. "You know what pisses me off about today, Carl? I've had to spend all of it running the hell away from you. No more."

He hadn't expected Kaylee to stand up to him, she could tell. The cockiness on his face faded slightly. "No, strike that. I might have *started* the day running away from you, but you know what? That changed. I ended running *to* somewhere at the end. Someplace I wanted to be. This is the place, and I don't really appreciate you being here. So you're going to leave and you're never, ever going to come back again. Not here, and not to me."

"Oh yeah?" Carl tried to sound tough.

One obstacle at a time, Kaylee told herself. After today, what couldn't she face? "Yeah. You want to have this out? Do it like a man and not like a baby. We'll do it the adult way, you and me. You need to steal a little girl's violin to protect you? Aw, poor widdle Carl."

Carl faltered and stopped swinging the violin. "I don't need—hey!"

Rosa had run up behind him and grabbed the case out of Carl's hand, dashing off to Ramon's side. Kaylee felt satisfaction at her opponent's bewilderment and advanced on him. He stumbled backward. "So let's be adults, Carl. What do you want? Money? Sorry, I don't have any. Yeah, I've got my dad's ATM card still, but the machines aren't working. What else could you want? Revenge? How, by beating up my friends? Very classy, picking on kids smaller than you. Want to beat me up? Fine. Give it a try, but yeah, keep in mind that my dad taught his army princess pretty well in the self-defense department."

"I bet your dad would be interested in hearing about where you've been all day."

She had her answer ready for that one. "So tell him. Tell him everything." At that invitation, he looked blank. "What's the matter? Don't want to? Oh, yeah, why, because he thinks you're Evil with a bad haircut? Oh, and the little fact that I was going to tell him first? Funny thing about being someone's victim, Carl. Most people step right up for the job. I made a whole freakin' career out of being your puppet, but a job is something you can quit. And walking away from it right now is the best thing I'm ever going to do." Carl seemed utterly flabbergasted at the words pouring out of her mouth. She took a step closer.

"So what, you think that's it?" he sputtered.

"No. I *know* that's it." She shook her head. Ever since she'd met him, he'd slowly played all his cards—wheedling, intimidation, blackmail. Now she was simply abandoning the game. "You've got nothing over me, Carl. Nothing. So go back to your buddy Annabelle and give her my love—but instead of the love part, tell her she can bite my butt. Oh, and before you do . . . "

Her fingers had been curling into a fist, one by one, thumb curled at the side—exactly the way Ramon had taught her earlier in the day. Keeping aim on her target, she had pulled back as she talked and, without warning, let a punch fly. A thousand aching flowers sprang from her muscles when her fist caught Carl squarely on the right cheekbone and eye. The much larger boy staggered backward and landed against the fence. Ramon hadn't warned her that popping some- one felt a little like pummeling her hand against a con- crete wall, but she ignored the sweet bloom of pain in her elbow and shoulder and followed up the punch with a second feint, just as Ramon had done earlier that afternoon to the lock-slamming woman in the car. Like Ramon, she meant to scare him.

When Carl flinched back, frightened, she knew she'd banished him for good from her list of torments. He was the boogeyman forever scared away by day- light, a phantom evaporated by the sun. He spat out a number of four-letter words as he rubbed the redden- ing spot on his face. "Jesus, Kaylee," he swore. "I thought we were talking like adults."

"Yeah, well, consider that good-bye from my inner child." She crossed her arms and waited, head cocked. Carl took the hint. He gathered himself to his feet, stumbled down the drive, and lurched around the cor- ner, running like a little kid.

Kaylee knew she wouldn't see him again.

Ramon still lay sprawled on the ground. "Are you okay?" she asked him, checking to see if his pupils were equally dilated. She didn't know what it would mean if they weren't, but from watching *ER* she'd picked up that mismatched pupils were a bad sign. They seemed okay. Ramon nodded. "Did he break anything? Do you need an ambulance? Do you have a concussion?"

Her barrage of questions brought a smile to Ra- mon's face. He shook his head and raised his hand.

What did he want? Was he trying to pull her down, to tell her something? He waved his fingers again when she started to kneel. "What?" she finally asked.

His lips worked out two slow words. "Help me." After a few more seconds, he tried again. "Help me up."

Ramon's hand wrapped around her wrist as she held on to his own. "All you ever had to do was ask," Kaylee told him.

7:29 P.M.

The blow to his head hadn't been that bad; Ramon had only been stunned for a moment. Yes, he told Kaylee, he could focus his eyes. No, he wasn't having a problem with bright lights. No, he didn't feel dizzy. No, he didn't think his skull had gotten a hairline fracture. Yes, Rosa's violin was okay.

Yes, he had thought Kaylee's performance had been, in a word, *money.* She decided it sounded good, whatever it meant.

They stood at the back door of her house, where in the kitchen everything was exactly as Kaylee had left it that morning, when she'd gotten Annabelle's phone call: Eggo waffle sitting half finished on her plate, a fly buzzing around its sticky syrup, her schoolbooks sitting on the edge of the kitchen table. They seemed relics of a completely different, ancient life. The one thing that had changed was a slip of paper sitting atop the books, upon which Ramon had scrawled some digits: his phone number.

"We better go," he told her, holding her hand for

the last time that day. "But . . . let me know, okay? Either way. If you wanna like, do something sometime, I'll do it. But I gotta know, either way, what you decide. . . . " His voice trailed off into uncertainty. Finally, after a struggle, Ramon gathered his courage and came out with what was on his mind. "Are you gonna tell your dad? Do you know what you're gonna say?"

"I don't know," Kaylee said, trying to be honest. "But I'll tell you the truth, either way. I swear. It's the best I can promise."

"Yeah."

It was an awkward moment. Neither of them wanted to say the word good-bye. "Can we *go* already?" Rosa blurted out from the bottom of the steps. "Before another of your army princess's thug friends comes around and beats the crap out of you?" Kaylee laughed, and wandered with Ramon down to the bottom of the steps and around to the drive. "I mean, *dang*," Rosa continued to complain, "you don't get those kinds of punks in *our* neighborhood."

"Invite me to one of your concerts, please?" Kaylee asked her.

She thought she saw the girl grimace, but in the proper little lady voice, Rosa replied, "Of course! That would be very nice! Thank you for a lovely day and *let's go already!*" With a warning glare at her brother, she stomped down the drive, violin tucked under her arm.

"She don't mean that," Ramon said. "The being mean part, that is. She's—"

"Yeah. I spent enough time with your sister today to know what she is. She's ten. And she's special, Ramon. Real special. So hey." Kaylee squeezed his arm. "Ask

Manuel for help when you can use it. It's not that hard."

"Yeah," he said, very quietly. "I know."

"Do I gotta pretend I gotta pee again? I could get an *Oscar* for it, by now!" Rosa yelled from the street. Ramon turned, smiled wryly, and lifted his hand. Not *good-bye*. Not *see ya later*. Just a hand, and the sight of his eyes wrenching themselves from hers, then the slope of his neck as he ducked and turned away. It wouldn't be the last time she saw him, she reminded herself. No matter what she decided to do, it wouldn't be the last time.

The boy was about to round the Scotts' shrubbery and vanish when Kaylee yelled from her position beside the porch, "Ramon!" He turned, surprised. "Honeysuckle," she called out. His eyebrows crunched together. He didn't understand. "When you talk. Your words—that's what they smell like to me. Honeysuckle . . . "

Kaylee's last words trailed off so softly that she knew Ramon couldn't have heard them, but he'd caught enough to understand. He nodded. After a second, his face lit up. Even if it were to be the last time she saw the boy, Kaylee could bear the memory of that final glimpse of his face, smiling from ear to ear, looking at her with a tenderness that surpassed anything she thought she could deserve.

How long did she stand there, head against the front porch pillar, gazing off after two figures she couldn't see? Long enough that the sky had darkened slightly above, putting on a rainbow display of colors as the sun neared the horizon, almost as if determined to provide the evening's entertainment for an entire section of the country without lights to read by—or televisions, or computers, or any of the hundred electrical gadgets they usually relied on. Maybe little crises like the blackout brought out the true essence of a person, Kaylee thought. Maybe they helped people find out whether they were determined or vague, strong or weak, honest or sneaky.

Helpful—or helpless.

So what kind of person was she? That was the question she had to decide in the next few minutes. It would be so easy to pretend to her father that she hadn't done anything out of the ordinary that day.

Yet she didn't think she'd admire herself very much for it. As she'd told Carl, she didn't need to run from lies anymore. She could run toward the truth, and embrace it. If there were consequences . . . well, she could face them, one at a time.

From the street came a crunch of tires and the roar of a mighty engine. The Jeep's headlights were so intensely bright in the dusk that Kaylee had to hold up a hand to shield her eyes from their glare. Against the day's backdrop, she was alone in the spotlights now, with no supporting players. Only her performance would count from this point.

She intended to make it matter.

CHLOE,
QUEEN OF DENIAL

NAOMI NASH

If you're reading this note, you're probably in the middle of the desert pulling it from the vulture-plucked bones of someone who used to be named Chloe Bryce.

Or maybe you're my poor, grieving parents who sent me to die in Egypt. A month at the Tomb of Tekhen and Tekhnet will look really good on your college resume, you said. Satisfied now, guys? Maybe you two didn't know I'd end up facing risks that would make Indiana Jones think twice—baths only every ten days, blistering heat, ancient tombs, mummies, a cursed bracelet . . . Of course, I did manage to kiss the dig's one hot guy—so you can console yourselves that I died somewhat happy!

YOU ARE *SO* CURSED!

NAOMI NASH

High school's a dog eat dog world, but Vickie Marotti has an edge. Scorned by the jocks and cheerleaders? Misunderstood by the uptight vice principal? No problem. Not when you're an adept street magician, hexing bullies who dare harass you or your outcast friends!

But then cute and popular upperclassman Gio Carson recognizes the truth: Vick's no more a witch than she is class president. Her dark curses are nothing more than smoke and mirrors. Will he tell the world, or will it be their little secret? Vick's about to learn a valuable lesson: that real magic lies in knowing your true friends.

Got Fangs?
Katie Maxwell

I used to think all I wanted was to have a normal life. You know, where I could be one of the crowd and blend in, so no one would know just how different I am. But now I'm stuck in the middle of Hungary with my mom, working for a traveling fair with psychics, magicians, and other really weird people, and somehow, blending in with this crowd doesn't look so good.

Fortunately, there's Benedikt. Yeah, he may be a vampire, but he has a motorcycle, and best of all, he doesn't think I'm the least bit freaky. So I'm supposed to redeem his soul—if his kisses are anything to go by, my new life may not be quite as bad as I imagined.

Didn't want this book to end?

There's more waiting at **www.smoochya.com**:

Win FREE books and makeup!
Read excerpts from other books!
Chat with the authors!
Horoscopes!
Quizzes!
